HALLOWS END

A Sarah Chase Novel

LEO CRAVEN

DEDICATION

To my loving wife, Sadeana. Thank you for being my inspiration.

To my sons, Trace and Nick. May you never give up on your dreams.

To all my other wonderful friends and family. I am truly appreciative of all you have given to me over the years.

I am blessed to have each and every one of you in my life.

CHAPTER 1

March 27, 1033 AD - A small group of campfires and tents formed an outpost in the midst of the dense, Northern Scotland forest. Lord Artair, Guardian of the North, sat in the largest tent marked by a worn yellow flag bearing the Kingdom's symbol, a red lion. The Scottish Lord was waiting for the "sign in the sky" that had been prophesied by an elderly witch who'd burned at the stake under the King's laws. This "sign", according to the witch, would reveal the birthplace of a child who would bear unprecedented power.

While most denounced her heresy as madness, King Malcolm II took notice and had the witch tortured for more information before allowing her to die. In between her cries of agony, the witch told of an ancient prophecy that involved the re-born child of Lucifer and Navaia, the "Fallen Ones". She predicted that this child of prophecy would be born within a fortnight of the spring solstice in the land of the Scotts.

LEO CRAVEN

King Malcolm II assembled all of the lords of the land shortly after learning of the prophecy, and divulged such secrets to them that some questioned whether he had gone mad. The King spoke of great and powerful societies that existed tens of thousands of years before, an ancient weapon that had wiped out entire kingdoms, and of a prophecy that would bring about the rise of a demon race. King Malcolm II explained that it must be mortal man that secured this child. Although Lord Artair didn't believe in demons and prophecies, he was a loyal servant to the King and always followed orders.

A young soldier burst into Artair's tent. "My Lord…the sky….you must come!" the soldier stuttered.

Artair stood up from his chair. He was tall, standing at 6'3, with broad shoulders and strong, dark features. Without a word, he ran past the soldier and out of the tent to see a magnificent blue light shining down on the earth, not more than five leagues from where they had set up camp. While the witch had been correct in her prediction of the light in the sky, Artair was not yet convinced that it had anything to do with the birth of a child or a prophecy.

The Guardian of the North commanded his men to pack up their base so they could start heading toward the light. If there were, indeed, demon spies lurking in the forests of Northern Scotland, Artair was certain he could reach the child before any of them. However, he also acknowledged that if anyone else were searching the sky for signs, its whereabouts certainly posed no mystery.

HALLOWS END

After every league traveled, Artair commanded
two soldiers to stay behind in order to cover the trail they
were blazing. The soldiers' orders were to build a beacon
and light it on fire at the first sign of trouble. If an enemy
were in pursuit, he wanted as much warning as possible.
His army, as it stood, barely numbered 200 men, and they
would be unable to fight off a large-scale attack for very
long.

It was nearing midnight by the time Artair and his
soldiers approached a small village located at the base of a
magnificent mountain range. There were a dozen homes,
one of which had the light from the sky shining upon it.
Artair looked around and determined that he and his men
were the first to arrive. He dismounted from his horse,
and commanded his soldiers to begin setting up
fortifications.

Artair summoned two of his soldiers and walked
toward the house that had been marked by the sky. As
they approached, he could hear the screams of a woman in
labor. He knocked on the door twice. "I, Lord Artair of
the Northern Kingdom under the command of King
Malcolm II, proclaim my intention to enter your
home," he stated, with the authority of the King himself.
There was no answer from within so he proceeded to
enter.

The inside of the hut was comprised of one room
which had been divided into two sections with a cloth
partition that hung from the ceiling. Lord Artair cautiously
made his way past the screen and saw two women, one
lying on a bed and the other, who appeared to be a

midwife, holding a wet cloth to the laboring mother's forehead.

The midwife looked up to greet Artair. "We were expecting you, my Lord," she said. "My name is Olwyn, and this," she looked down at the bed on which the other woman lay, "is Tyra." Artair was speechless. Not only had the light in the sky brought them to the birthplace of a child, but now he found himself in the company of two Druid witches, as indicated by the marks on their foreheads.

Olwyn rose from Tyra's bedside and approached Artair. Olwyn was an attractive woman, though she was clearly past her child-bearing years. Her blue eyes seemed to reflect off her white hair as she spoke to him. "Do you know what we are?" she asked.

"I believe the symbols you bear on your flesh indicate that you are witches," Artair responded, showing some level of discomfort around the subject. He had been told by one of the King's guards that the witch who told them of the prophecy bore the same mark, a crescent moon with a trinity knot.

"We are members of a small order of witches in these forests, and we mean no harm to the soldiers of King Malcolm," Olwyn assured him, bowing her head slightly.

"As we mean no harm to you," Artair replied. He wasn't convinced that he spoke for his kingdom with those words, but he intended to honor them none the less.

"Your pagan beliefs are of no concern to me tonight," he continued. "We are simply here to protect the child."

"Ah, yes. You believe this child to be the spiritual descendant of Lucifer and Navaia, don't you?"

"I'm not sure of the things you speak of. My orders are simply to secure the safety of the child and await the arrival of our King's army." Artair lowered his eyes to Tyra. He studied her, noticing her long golden hair and green eyes. Her beauty was unmatched by any other woman that he had ever gazed upon.

"Please, my Lord," Tyra pleaded from her bed. Artair's dire resolve softened for just a moment as he drew closer to the expectant mother. "My baby will be here soon. Protect my village from the evil that approaches and both my child and I will follow you…anywhere."

Artair's dark brown eyes momentarily glossed over as he searched Tyra's face for a glimpse into her heart. For a brief second he became very aware that he could fall in love with this woman. "My lady," he said, bowing slightly while maintaining eye contact. "I would give my very life to protect you and this child."

Tyra looked back at him momentarily and then screamed out in agony. "The child is coming," Olwyn stated, returning to Tyra's side as Artair stepped over to the other side of the cloth and waited. The next few hours brought only intermittent moaning as the labor carried on through the night. An hour before dawn, Artair looked out the window to see one of his soldiers running toward the hut.

"My Lord!" the soldier announced as he entered through the doorway, "The fires have been lit."

Artair looked away from the window with a concerned look on his face. "Do we know what approaches, Diarmad?"

"Our men report an army of gray soldiers in the thousands approaching, my Lord." Diarmad was one of Artair's most trusted soldiers. He was a younger lad, barely 19 years of age, yet he already had the build of a man with broad shoulders, dark brown hair and steel grey eyes. Artair often thought to himself that should he ever have a son, he hoped that boy would turn out like Diarmad.

"Thousands?" Artair questioned in disbelief. "How could they have entered our Kingdom unnoticed with such numbers?"

"The demon army has ways to elude the eyes of mortal men, my Lord," Olwyn interjected from behind the cloth. Artair was annoyed with the witch's eavesdropping.

"Demons!" Artair scoffed. "Merely men in gray armor!" He shouted loudly enough so that Olwyn would hear his response, though she clearly could hear him just fine. "What flag does this army bear?" he asked Diarmad.

HALLOWS END

"They bear a symbol none of our scouts recognize, my Lord, and..." there was hesitation now in Diarmad's voice, "they do not sport gray armor. It is their skin that is gray...like ash."

Artair allowed Diarmad's words to resonate in his mind as he considered his next plan of action. His 200 men would be annihilated by an army of thousands and there was no chance that King Malcolm II's army could reach them in time.

"Diarmad," Artair spoke, "send riders to the south, southeast and southwest. They are to carry a message to King Malcolm II that we have secured the child of prophecy, but that an enemy army approaches." Diarmad acknowledged his Lord's orders and exited swiftly.

Shortly after Diarmad had left, Tyra unleashed a fury of screams that were loud enough to be heard throughout the entire village. Artair waited impatiently, hoping that the child would be born soon so they could vacate the village in time to avoid the army of gray soldiers. The distinct sounds of a newborn baby having its first taste of the outside world started to fill the small hut. However, they were quickly drowned out by another round of Tyra's feverish yells.

"What's wrong?" Artair shouted out with concern.

"Nothing," Olwyn responded calmly. "Lady Tyra is having another." He was startled by her announcement and remained still. Several questions raced through his mind, but he thought better than to interrupt the mid-wife while she was helping with the delivery. After a short period of time he heard the cries of a second child. "May I now come over and see them?" Artair asked.

"You may," replied Olwyn from behind the cloth.

He lifted the curtain and saw two babies lying in a small crib next to Tyra. "They are beautiful," Artair said out loud. Just like their mother, he thought to himself.

Tyra opened her eyes half way, looked at Artair and smiled. "Thank you," she said softly and then returned to her sleep.

Artair and Olwyn stepped outside the hut while Tyra rested. He looked at the sun rising and turned to Olwyn. "I thought the prophecy only spoke of one child? What does the birth of two mean?"

"I do not know," she said with a smile. "It appears that the unborn child of the Fallen Ones has returned as two souls rather than one."

"My King spoke of a birthmark," Artair continued as he tried to make sense of the event. "Something about the child bearing the symbol of two ancient races. Do either of them have a birthmark?"

Olwyn took a deep breath and replied. "Each girl bears one of the marks. The first born, Avonmora, bears the mark of Navaia's race, the Atlantians. The second child, Keara, bears the symbol of Lucifer's people, the Lemurians."

"Atlantis. Lemuria. These are mythic places you speak of," he scoffed.

"These myths are about to become very real for all of us, my Lord," Olwyn responded. "The demon hordes will be here soon and your King Malcolm," she paused with a deep sigh, "does not want the children protected for long. As soon as he has them in his possession he will have them killed."

"Why would King Malcolm II want to have innocent babies murdered?" Artair retorted.

"Because King Malcolm, like all kings before him, fears power that is greater than his own," Olwyn replied. Her conviction silenced Artair momentarily while he measured her words. However, he refused to trust the words of a witch over his own King's.

"Demon army or not, my men will not be able to hold them off. We must leave immediately and hope that their army cannot track us into the dense forests of our own lands."

"They will not allow us to leave, my Lord."

"Lord Artair!" shouted a booming voice from behind the door of the hut. The door flew open and in walked a tall, stout man with a graying beard and hardened face. "The enemy's army approaches at a pace I've never seen, sire. They have already sent scouts out requesting your presence in order to negotiate our surrender."

Sir Gordan's words filled the room with tension. Artair let out a deep, angry sigh as he looked back at his second in command. "How much time do we have?"

"I'm afraid there's no time to coordinate an escape." Sir Gordan was extremely upset with himself that he hadn't been able to give his lord more warning. He had been Artair's second in command for over ten years and had never let him down until this day.

"Well," Artair said, shrugging his shoulders. "I guess it's time for me to see what these demons look like."

Artair and Gordan walked toward the command tent which was little more than a furlong from Tyra's home. In front of the tent stood two extremely large figures with skin as gray as storm clouds and both bearing massive battle axes. Artair walked up and addressed the shorter of the two soldiers who was still a good six inches taller than he. "Where is the commander of your army?"

"He awaits you in your tent, Lord," the demon soldier replied. Artair was rather surprised by the congenial tone of the demon soldier though his instincts were to kill them both and take hostage the man or creature that awaited him inside.

"Lord Artair, Guardian of Northern Scotland!" the Demon exclaimed as Artair walked into the tent. In contrast to the soldiers outside, the demon stood well under six feet and wore a black cloak from his neck down to his black boots. His facial hair was perfectly groomed and he spoke with a charming yet devious tone in his voice. "I can honestly say," he continued with a bow, "that it is an honor to meet you."

With a raised eyebrow, Artair responded. "While I appreciate the, um, pleasantries, I'm not terribly excited to see your army in my King's forest. What brings you to this village, demon?"

"My name is Dominious," he responded, "descendant of the great Lord Brakkus, and royal advisor to King Renner." Dominious paused, giving Artair time to recognize that he was in the presence of royalty.

"And what can I do for you, Dominious?" Artair replied, unimpressed with the demon's introduction.

"You know what it is we've come for, Lord Artair," Dominious said a little less congenially. "I am here to negotiate the delivery of the child in exchange for my army leaving this village peacefully."

"I don't know what you're talking about, demon. My King's army approaches with haste and should arrive by mid-day. I think it is best that you leave before they arrive." Artair stared into Dominious's black eyes, hoping his bluff would work.

"I see." Dominious gave an unconvinced look as he stroked his narrow beard with his right hand. "Unfortunately for you, Lord Artair, I have received word that King Malcolm's army is nowhere close to these lands. Now, if you prefer, we can kill your soldiers, rape the women and burn this village to the ground. However, my time is precious and I'd prefer the path of least resistance." Dominious finished his words while Artair stewed in silent rage.

"I'm afraid you have no choice, Lord Artair. My army's numbers are far too great for your men to defeat. You and I both know that I will be leaving with the child one way or another." Dominious made his way to the tent's entrance, keeping a significant distance between him and Artair. "If you would like to avoid the pointless slaughter of your men and the people of this village, then you will bring the child to me within the hour."

Artair said nothing as the demon made his exit. He stared across the desk in the middle of his tent while he determined his next move. Dominious was right; Artair knew his men could not hold back the demon army. However, he considered that Dominious also had no knowledge of the second child born that day. Tyra would not willingly give up one of her daughters and Artair could not bear to ask her, but it seemed the only chance they had for survival. With a desperate mind, he returned to Tyra's home.

"I know what you are considering, Lord Artair," Olwyn said to him as he gazed upon Tyra, still sleeping. "I am not a seer, but I can sense your thoughts. You believe that handing over one of the children to the demon army is the only way to save us."

HALLOWS END

Artair didn't have the energy to act bothered about the fact that Olwyn was reading his mind. Instead he spoke to her openly. "My men and I can't protect you and your village. The demon army will bring a reign of terror too horrible to fathom if I do nothing."

"Then you must do what your heart is telling you," Olwyn leaned forward and placed her hand on Artair's arm. "She will forgive you," Olwyn said, referring to Tyra.

Artair knew that Olwyn could see that he had feelings already growing for Tyra. "I hope so," he replied, looking over at the two babies. "How do I choose?"

"The demons are a proud race, never forgetting that their roots were originally planted in the kingdom of Lemuria. By giving them Keara, the child that bears the Lemurian symbol, your deception has a much better chance for success."

After several minutes passed by, Artair let out a deep sigh and picked Keara up from her crib. She made a slight noise and then fell quickly back to sleep as Artair made his way back to his tent. Every step he took with Keara in his arms was pure torture.

"You've made a wise decision, Lord Artair," Dominious said as he held out his arms to receive Keara.

Artair hesitated as he handed the beautiful child over to the demon. He could feel his heart break at the thought of what kind of life the girl had in store for her. Artair vowed to save the child as soon as he was able to get Tyra and Avonmora to safety. "My King will hunt your army down and kill every last one of you," he growled.

"Of course he will," Dominious snorted. The demon turned Keara over and adjusted the blanket she was wrapped in so he could inspect the birthmark on her back. Dominious looked slightly confused when he saw only the symbol of Lemuria. He looked up at Artair and could tell that the Scotsman was hiding something from him. He considered questioning Artair about the missing birthmark, but decided it would be better to take his leave. Dominious grinned and started to make his way to exit.

"I have your word that this village and my men are safe from you army then?" Artair asked as he blocked Dominious' exit.

"You have my word, Lord Artair. This village and your men will remain unscathed."

As soon as Dominious had left, Artair began issuing orders to his men. Most of his soldiers were to remain in the village under the command of Gordan until the demon army was well out of sight. Then, Gordan was to leave two scouts in the village while the rest of them joined Artair en route to the Lord's castle.

Artair rode with a dozen of his best men back to Tyra's home where he found that Olwyn had done an effective job of calming Tyra enough so that they were prepared to leave. Tyra would not even look at Artair as she boarded the supplies wagon with Avonmora in her arms. "I know you have no desire to speak to me," he said to her, "but I swear that once you and Avonmora are safe, I will find Keara and bring her back to you." She said nothing in return.

Artair's castle was a solid three days journey, made longer by his desire to avoid the towns and villages along the way. If any of his fellow countrymen saw him or his soldiers, it could put those individuals at risk of interrogation by their enemies. As the night came upon them, Artair and his men made camp. There had been no sign of Gordan or his army, and he now feared that Dominious had gone back on his word.

It was nearing midnight as the full moon shone down upon the sleeping soldiers and the tent in which Tyra, Olwyn and Avonmora slumbered. Artair and two of his other men kept post. "My Lord," whispered Diarmad. "There is something beyond those trees." Diarmad cocked his head toward a dark patch in the forest to the right of their camp.

Artair knew of what Diarmad spoke of as he had been holding his sword tightly for the last hour in anticipation of what was approaching. He nodded to Diarmad in agreement and then motioned with his hand to direct the young soldier to move forward with him. The patch of forest they now encroached upon was only a few wagon lengths in front of them. Just as they neared their destination, a shrieking howl came from the darkness.

Three giant black wolves bounded from the trees and headed directly toward them. Artair turned to his soldiers who were waking up in haste. "Protect the ladies' tent!" he commanded as he plunged his sword into the heart of the first beast. The wolf let out a horrible yelp and withdrew back into the forest. Artair could not see well in the dark, but swore that he saw the wolf retreat running upright.

More beasts came upon them as Artair continued to strike at them with a warrior's rage. He was determined to keep Tyra and Avonmora alive and knew that their only chance of survival was his blade. A third wave of wolves came at them and he began to fear they might be overtaken. Two of his men had already fallen, and he could no longer see Diarmad by his side. Suddenly, Artair heard screams coming from the direction of the ladies' tent.

Despite his soldiers' best efforts, the wolves had broken through their line. Artair rushed toward the screams only to see Olwyn try, unsuccessfully, to slash at one of the wolves with a dagger. She died instantly as the beast closed its jaws around her neck, grabbed her arms with its own and ripped her body apart. Artair's eyes grew wide, realizing that these were not mere wolves they were being attacked by. "Werewolves!" he said aloud in disbelief.

The beast didn't have time to turn around before Artair delivered a deadly blow with his sword into the werewolf's spine. Artair had scarcely removed his sword from the creature's back when he heard another scream from only a short distance away. "No!!!" he heard Tyra cry out.

Artair immediately turned toward her direction and saw the outline of Tyra's body thrown to the ground by one of the beasts. Artair rushed to her side and found her crying uncontrollably. She had suffered a nasty bite on her left arm, but it was not pain that forced Tyra's tears. "They took her!" she cried hysterically. "They took Avonmora!"

No longer giving any thought to the battle behind him, Artair quickly mounted his horse and pursued the werewolf into the forest. Though his pace was limited, he could hear Avonmora's muffled cries grow louder, giving him hope that he was gaining on her captor. Just then, two werewolves sprang from the shadows and knocked Artair from his horse. He reached for the dagger by his side and thrust it with all his might into the first werewolf's jaw, spewing its blood in all directions. This bought him enough time to reach for his sword that had fallen a few feet away. The second werewolf made its move to attack, but Artair already had the tip of his sword near the wolf's neck.

"Stand up, you bastard!" he commanded the wolf. Artair wasn't sure if he had gone completely insane expecting the wolf to understand him. The werewolf snarled as it slowly stood upright. Artair was thankful his sword filled the distance between him and the beast. The werewolf stood well over a foot taller than the Scottish Lord and had a massive frame that looked primed for combat.

"Do you speak, beast?" Artair questioned, pushing the sword slightly harder into the werewolf's throat. The werewolf didn't respond, but he could tell that it understood the question. "Tell me where your pack is taking the child!" Artair stepped forward slightly, forcing the werewolf to its knees under the pressure of his blade.

"You will never see the child again," the werewolf responded in a gnarled dialect that Artair could barely understand.

"Oh, I will," Artair stared into the werewolf's glowing yellow eyes. "Even if it means killing every last one of your hellish race to do so!" He thrust his sword in a cold rage and decapitated the fowl beast.

"My Lord!" said a voice behind him. Artair turned to see Diarmad approach him. Though the night weighed heavy with tragedy, Artair was glad to see the young soldier had survived. "Should we pursue the beasts?" Diarmad asked.

"No. We cannot catch them in the darkness. We will return to the camp, collect our wits, and begin pursuit tomorrow."

When they reached the camp, Artair was distraught to find Tyra shaking uncontrollably. The bite on her arm was festering and out of her mouth came a white, foamy substance. Artair knelt down and tried to hold her still while tears filled his eyes. He knew if they did not begin their pursuit of Avonmora in the morning, the chances of them ever finding her were bleak.

However, he could not choose the life of a child over this woman whom he was falling in love with.

"Diarmad," Artair spoke as he looked up with a desperate look in his eyes. "Pack up the camp. We must return to the village now!" Diarmad understood and immediately gathered their remaining soldiers. Artair looked upon Tyra, still shivering fiercely as she drifted out of consciousness. "I will not let you die," he whispered softly.

CHAPTER 2 (Current Day)

The bouncer stopped Stanley from entering the club by placing his over-sized hand directly on Stanley's chest.

"Sorry, Buddy. I don't think so," the bouncer said condescendingly. He stood about six inches taller than Stanley and had biceps the size of most men's heads.

"Are you sure you can't make an exception?" Stanley asked. His left hand shook slightly as he raised it to his shirt pocket and pulled out a $100 bill.

"Whatever, old man," the bouncer laughed. He took Stanley's money and let him pass.

Stanley proceeded to walk through the door of the nightclub and was greeted by an orgy of young, barely clothed bodies that spanned from the entrance to the dance floor. As he made his way to the bar, women did their best to avoid eye contact with him, all of them hoping that he wouldn't try to make a move. Stanley was in his 50's, balding, and was about 40 pounds overweight. To make matters worse, he was wearing a short-sleeved dress shirt with a tie that made him look like a low budget accountant.

"Whoa! You lost, Pops?" the bartender mocked him. She was a tiny little thing, with short brown hair, several piercings, and a rose tattoo around her right eye.

"Nope, doing just fine, thank you," he said with an innocent smile. "Can I get a Bud Light please?"

"Bud Light?" The bartender's eyes nearly popped out of her head. "Are you fucking kidding me, ol' man?"

"Is that not hip?" Stanley responded with a pathetic, almost puppy dog innocence.

The bartender looked at him, but rather than continue to break his balls, she decided to take pity on him instead. "Listen, if you want to try and blend in at a place like this you better drink like the locals." She quickly grabbed a shot glass and filled it with what appeared to be vodka. "Start with this", she shouted as the music got even louder, "and burn the goddamned tie!"

Stanley took the shot glass and placed it on his lips. He stared at the bartender's ass while she was turned around making him a drink. The beast within him stirred as he allowed his thoughts to delve into the darker corners of his mind. With a deep breath Stanley shot back his head and downed it. After the burning sensation in his throat subsided, he reached for his collar and took off his tie, placing it on the counter.

"I'll take care of that for you." The bartender grabbed the tie and replaced the shot glass with a glass full of some kind of pink alcohol on the rocks. Stanley considered the bartender as a possible option for his evening's agenda, glancing briefly at her chest and picturing the perfect heart that beat within it. "Enjoy!" she shouted.

"Thanks," Stanley shouted back. Though the bartender was his type, he decided that choosing an employee of the club might create too much of a trail. Besides, it was Friday, the night was young, and there were plenty of good options surrounding him.

He took another $100 out of his wallet and left it for her. "Keep the change." Stanley could hear the bartender squeal with joy as he walked away from the bar. He figured it would be good to have a friend in the place in case he needed any information later; or if the night didn't go as planned.

The dance floor was packed with writhing bodies, but Stanley quickly determined that wasn't his scene. He was already beginning to sweat and didn't want to become so repulsive that none of the girls would even talk to him. Instead he made his way over to the booths and spotted one with several attractive girls sporting short dresses, and more importantly, an open seat. Stanley walked up to the booth and casually introduced himself.

"Hello," Stanley said. None of the girls made eye contact or any attempt at stopping their conversations to acknowledge him.

"My name is Stanley," he continued. "Do, uh, any of you know what this drink is called?" He held up his glass and smiled, doing his best to appear completely clueless and pathetic. It was a method that had worked well for him in the past so he figured why mess with an effective formula.

"Hey, Stanley," the tall brunette in the middle of the booth stopped her conversation to look up. "Fuck off!"

Stanley took a step back from the table and did his best to look dejected.

"Hey, take it easy on the guy, Amber," a girl wearing a red top with short black hair said. She looked up at Stanley and gave him a half smile. "What you doin' here in this club, Stanley?"

"I have no idea." He smiled back at her. "I'm just trying to avoid spending another evening alone in my apartment…pathetic, huh?"

"Tell you what, Stanley," the girl in red continued as Amber rolled her eyes. "As long as you promise not to hit on any of us, you can hang here until our other friend arrives." She motioned at the open seat to her left and scooted over slightly toward the blonde girl on her right.

Stanley sat down, careful to leave plenty of space so as not to come off creepy. The girl in red told him her name was Keisha and then proceeded to introduce him to the rest of her party. Upon meeting all of the girls in the booth, Stanley was immediately taken with Emily, a petite young woman with short blonde hair and bright blue eyes. He could feel the hairs both on and under his skin stiffen as he took in her scent.

"So, Stanley," Emily spoke up. "I noticed you're wearing a wedding ring; why didn't your wife come out with you?"

"I'm afraid she passed away about six months ago, Emily," he said, pausing and becoming emotional. "I know it's time that I start moving on, but I can't seem to bring myself to take it off," he continued as he looked longingly at the ring. Stanley added a few more details to the story and quickly gained the sympathy of Emily and most of the girls at the table.

After some small talk and a round of drinks, Stanley decided to make his move before the girls' other friend arrived. "So, do all of you live in the city?" he asked. Stanley could tell that Amber suspected he was up to something, but the rest of the girls took the question in stride as just another topic of their conversation.

"Most of us," Keisha answered. "Except for Emily. She's the only one who's too good to live in the city!" Keisha laughed and tapped Emily's bare shoulder. Stanley couldn't help but take notice of the light touch and almost drooled at the thought of his own hand touching Emily's bare skin.

"Ah, you're lucky," he said, looking at Emily. "City life's convenient, but there's nothing like having your own home to return to every night." By now, Stanley knew for certain that Emily was his choice for the evening. He proceeded to envision what her naked body must look like under her silver dress while the other girls began to banter back and forth as to whether life in the city or suburbs was better. After a few more minutes of the conversation, the girls' other friend, Monica, showed up.

"Thank you so much, ladies, for your company," Stanley said as he immediately got up from the booth. "You have been most gracious to this old man tonight." He exchanged a few parting words with the group of girls and then made his way to the exit. Monica sat down and ordered herself a drink while the rest of the girls filled her in on the story of Stanley.

Stanley walked out of the nightclub and headed to his car in the parking lot across the street. For the next few hours, he sat in his blue Chevy Malibu while he patiently watched the club's exit for any sign of Emily. Stanley could feel the pull of the moon and his desires to transform taking over as his mind repeatedly planned out his next steps over and over again. Finally, at about 1:30 AM, Emily and Keisha walked through the club's exit together and made their way to the line of taxis.

LEO CRAVEN

The girls' taxi dropped Keisha off first and then Emily as Stanley followed closely behind. Emily lived in an older, quaint part of Portland where sidewalks had cracked over the years from the large roots of oaks and maples. There was a short, white picket fence surrounding the front yard and several unkempt rose bushes that had begun taking over one side of her front porch. Emily fumbled around in her purse, digging for her keys and then walked in.

Lust and hunger fueled Stanley's mind as he sat in his car and imagined Emily walking into her bedroom and undressing. In his younger days Stanley would have made an effort to seduce Emily, or at least rape her before he ate her heart. These days, however, his sexual urges waned in favor of satisfying his hunger as quickly as possible.

Stanley drove around the neighborhood for a few minutes, then spotted a grade school with a well-hidden parking area. He salivated with maniacal anticipation as he got out of his car, removed his clothing and placed it, neatly folded, in the backseat. All of the seats were covered in plastic and he had several towels and baby wipes handy in order to clean himself up afterwards. There was something perversely erotic for Stanley about forcing himself to stay calm and methodical while his insides were on the edge of rupturing.

Under the sky he stood, naked, his pale white body reflecting the moon above. The night was warm and humid, giving Stanley's skin a greasy feel that would actually make his changing slightly less painful. Unlike shape shifters who could transition from their natural state to their desired form peacefully, a werewolf's transformation is violent. He once heard a fellow werewolf describe it as if needles poked their way through all of the pores in his body while every bone was broken and reset a dozen times. Stanley actually felt that description was a bit of an understatement.

As he looked to the moon above, Stanley had a single doubt enter his swelling brain: "What if Dr. Nemitz finds out"? Dr. Nemitz had taken Stanley in when he had nowhere to go and had saved him from certain death at the hands of the Order. It was also Dr. Nemitz who allowed him to leave Hallows End under the promise that he would no longer feed on humans to satisfy his hunger.

For a brief second Stanley considered putting his clothes back on and returning to the quiet little life he had lead for the last twelve months since leaving Hallows End. The thought, however, of remaining in this weaker, hungry state was too awful for Stanley to fathom. He looked up to the moon and allowed his ancestral instincts to take over.

Coarse, dark hair began sprouting all over Stanley's body. Razor sharp nails emerged from both his hands and feet while his skin stretched to make room for the rapid growth of bulging muscles. The pain became unbearable for Stanley. His spine crackled as it bowed and his jaw bone extended three times its original length with a loud "pop".

"Cursed my species is!" he growled as the final stages of his transformation took place. His teeth grew jagged and long, and his eyes went from their usual pale blue to an intense, dark yellow.

Stanley Jones no longer resembled his weak, human form. Instead, standing in his place, was a fierce ancestor of the immortal werewolf race. A species who was created by the Goddess Armedes herself as an act of vengeance when she found her human lover, Lycanas, sleeping with a mortal girl. And, like all werewolves since Lycanas, Stanley was destined to exact vengeance in Armedes' name upon yet another innocent girl.

The back of Emily's house had a six-foot fence surrounding it that Stanley easily hurled himself over. He then made his way to the back patio where he hid in the shadows under her porch. Stanley quivered with devious intent as he began to simulate the sound of a whining pup. He knew it would only be a matter of time before Emily would come to him.

Emily couldn't hear Stanley's whines over the flushing of the toilet. She glanced at her toothbrush sitting on the side of the sink, but that seemed a little too daunting of a task for the evening. Instead, she simply rinsed with mouthwash for about ten seconds and decided that was good enough. With every step she took on her way to the bedroom the hallway spun a little bit harder. Emily stripped her clothes off and made her way to the bed, crashing on top of the covers.

After a few seconds the toilet stopped running, and the whining noise that Stanley was making began to resonate throughout the entire house. Emily figured it was one of the neighbor's dogs and she threw a pillow over her head to block out the noise. After about five minutes however, Stanley grew impatient and began making a bellowing whimpering sound that he knew Emily wouldn't be able to sleep through.

"Ugh!" Emily shouted out loud as she flung herself out of bed and grabbed her sheer pink nightgown. "Stupid Dog!" she proclaimed as she proceeded to the kitchen. Emily knew there was no way she was going to sleep through the racket, and figured the neighbor's dog had somehow made it into her backyard again. She turned the kitchen lights on and walked over to the sliding glass door that faced the backyard. Emily peered outside, but didn't see anything.

"What the hell?" she said out loud. Usually the dog came right up on to the porch and would stand there waiting until Emily came and got him. She waited about 30 seconds in silence and then threw up her arms in frustration. She started to head back to her bedroom when Stanley began making his whimpering noise again. Annoyed, she rolled her eyes, let out an exasperated sigh, and went back to the sliding glass door. This time she reached over and flipped the light switch on for the back patio.

Emily only had time for a half-scream as Stanley plunged through the door, sending shattered glass in every direction. He landed on top of her, crushing her rib cage and puncturing both of her lungs instantly. Emily clung to her final few breaths as Stanley took aim at her chest and buried his sharp claws deep into her sternum. She tried to scream, but there was no noise to be heard as the werewolf ripped her heart out and began feasting upon it.

Under the werewolf's weight, Emily convulsed violently for several seconds until the life finally left her eyes. Stanley slowed down to savor the last few remnants as he licked Emily's life blood from his hands. He breathed heavily from his exertion, looking around to make sure he hadn't missed any delicious pieces, and then just as suddenly as he had appeared, Stanley retreated back into the shadows.

CHAPTER 3

"Humph!" Sarah grunted as she struck the heavy bag hanging in the corner of the precinct's small, under-funded gymnasium. The black bag flew back and forth as she continued to throw a flurry of punches and kicks in its direction. Sweat beaded on every square inch of her perfectly toned body. Sarah only stood about 5'5, but she was conditioned perfectly for combat; the bag never stood a chance.

Even though it had been several years since her mixed martial arts days, Sarah continued to keep her body in pristine condition, knowing that her ability to survive depended on it. As a police detective, Sarah would admit that she didn't necessarily need the ability to disable someone with a single blow. Portland had its fair share of criminal activity, but in her seven years on the force (the last three of which she had spent as a detective), she had only drawn her gun a half dozen times and had never thrown a punch. Her "hobby" however, gave her ample opportunity to put all of her talents and skills to use.

Sarah walked over to the pull up bar and glanced in the mirror behind the rack of rusted dumbbells, allowing for a brief moment of satisfaction with herself. She was relentless in being the best in all facets of her life, and seldom took the time to commend herself for her efforts. Sarah adjusted her long dark hair in its ponytail, wiped a small white towel across her face and went back to her routine.

She was finishing up her second set of pull-ups when a younger officer in uniform came into the gym and interrupted her. He was shorter than the average guy, stocky, and had bright orange hair that he kept neatly parted on the side.

"Sarah Chase!" the officer yelled. "Chief wants to see you immediately."

"What for, Rogers?" Sarah grunted as she hit the mat to begin a set of push-ups. "Saturday's supposed to be my day off!" Sarah knew there wasn't such a thing as a 'day off' for a detective, but she liked to give the younger officers a hard time.

Rogers grinned briefly before he forced himself to become serious again. Most of the officers in the precinct had a thing for Detective Chase and struggled to keep shit-eating grins off their faces when they were in her presence. "Evidently," he continued, "there was another animal attack and it looks like the same whatever-the-fuck-it-is that killed the girl last month."

"Thanks, Bryan," Sarah choked out as she continued with her pushups. "Tell the Chief I'll be there in ten." Bryan excused himself, but still made sure to turn around for a casual peek at Sarah's ass while her back was turned. The guys had to be discreet around her since every one of them knew if she caught them they'd be sucking down their meals through a straw for the next month.

Sarah finished the last few reps she could muster and hit the shower. Although the news of an innocent girl's death certainly wasn't music to her ears, a sensation of excitement ran through her veins as she headed toward the locker room. Sarah hoped this latest attack would provide her with the final clues she needed to confirm what she believed had killed the young woman last month…a werewolf.

Since last month's attack, Sarah had identified three potential suspects, but hadn't yet been able to determine which of the three was the actual werewolf. Of course, as far as her Police Chief and the public was concerned, it was an animal attack; probably some runaway exotic pet that decided eating the citizens of Portland was a better option than starving.

She stripped off her gym clothes, grabbed her towel and walked into the shower. Her mind raced as she went over her plan for capturing and slaying the werewolf. Sarah knew the only sure-fire way to kill one of these monsters was to behead them. The notion that silver could be used to temporarily disable a werewolf was true, but decapitation seemed to be the only permanent solution that she had found so far.

It had been about 18 months since Sarah had become a vigilante "monster hunter" as she referred to it in her own head. Before that time she was a normal, level-headed police detective. Then, all hell broke loose when she tracked down a cult that was sacrificing young women.

She had arrived at the suspected whereabouts of the cult to find a group of vampire worshippers and, much to her surprise, a real vampire. Though she was ill-prepared for such a confrontation, Sarah was fortunate enough to encounter the vampire during the daylight (when vampires are at their weakest), and was able to blow away enough of its brains with her Glock that it couldn't regenerate.

Since then, Sarah had taken it upon herself to begin hunting down supernatural criminals and seeing that justice was served upon them. Thus far she had only a few kills to her credit, and had only seen vampires and werewolves. However, she acknowledged the possibility that other 'monsters' lurked in the shadows as well.

After showering, Sarah removed her towel and took a brief moment to admire her tattoos while standing in front of the locker room mirror. Most of the various works of art on her body she used to decorate the scars she had received during her early adulthood. Her favorite, however, was the ancient astrological symbol of the Pisces on her left shoulder blade. It was a birthday gift to herself when she turned 18, and it was the only link she had with her deceased mother, who had also been a Pisces. Sarah still longed to find out what had happened to her mother all those years ago. Why she had left. How she had died.

Suddenly, another female officer opened the door to the locker room, shaking Sarah from her temporary trip down memory lane. Sarah nodded politely to the younger officer, and then quickly walked over to her locker to get dressed. The Chief was the kind of guy that if you told him ten minutes and took eleven, you'd better be wearing earplugs.

CHAPTER 4

"Chase!" Chief Reynold's voice sounded off like a drill sergeant as Sarah walked through his door. He was an older man, probably in his late 60's, with a short white crew cut and an iron jaw. He was also as tough as police chiefs came. Last month, a 'crack head' had decided it would be a good idea to try and run out of the precinct while his arresting officer was looking the other direction. Chief Reynolds laid the guy out with one slight move of his forearm as the man attempted to run past him.

"Morning, Chief," Sarah responded to him with a smile that she knew would agitate him.

"Wipe that damn smile off your face, Chase!" he barked. "Your dad never smiled in my office and I don't want you starting any foolish trends!" Chief Reynolds acted the tough guy part, but in truth, he was a softy when it came to Sarah. The Chief had been very close to her step-father and viewed her as his own daughter.

"Sorry, Chief," she responded, trying to hide her grin.

"No, you're not," he replied, this time half smiling himself. "Would you please figure out what kind of fucking animal this is that's making midnight snacks out of the citizens of Portland?"

"I'm on it, Chief," Sarah answered, again being careful to keep her answers short. She could tell he was grumpy this morning and figured his wife had probably nagged him to death before he had gotten to work. His wife, Peggy, was actually a very sweet woman and a saint for putting up with him for all these years. However, she did like to pester him in the morning with a lot of 'Honey Do's'. Sarah knew this because she had lived with them for a few months during her senior year after her step-father had passed away from cancer.

"Then go take care of it!" Chief Reynolds motioned her toward the door while he picked up the phone and pretended he had something more important to do. "And do it before the damn animal rights activists get involved!"

Sarah jumped into her black Camaro and flew out of the police station's parking lot. When she arrived at the crime scene, Sarah walked right past the handful of reporters standing in front of Emily's house. It seemed that the vultures were all eager for an update on the "killer beast" that was hunting the residents of Portland. Fortunately for her, Chief Reynolds was a control freak who didn't like any of his officers talking to the press, so she happily avoided them whenever possible. Sarah was just about inside the house when she noticed Brad out of the corner of her eye. He was standing in the far corner of the front yard taking statements, probably from neighbors.

She hesitated ever so slightly. Brad was a tall, handsome officer, and was a few years younger than Sarah. He wasn't quite the fitness freak she was, but he definitely stayed in shape. It was supposed to have been just a one night fling, but instead, it had turned into six months of meeting up in bars on the weekends and a few late night booty calls. Sarah wasn't in love with Brad, but he was the closest thing she had ever had to a relationship; or even a close friend.

"Hey, Chase! You waiting for an invitation?" Sarah turned her attention to the doorway and saw Harris approaching her. Eugene Harris was a fellow detective who had been on the force for over 35 years. He was supposedly planning to retire this year, but he had been saying that for the past five.

"I didn't know you worked on Saturdays, Harris," Sarah joked as she walked through the doorway of Emily's house.

"I don't," Harris replied, his intense brown eyes doing their best to look around the house for clues and avoid contact with Sarah's. "I just figured I'd show up and babysit until you got here. I suppose you already know the details?"

HALLOWS END

"Young woman in her early 20's gets attacked and killed by some wild animal in her kitchen. Sounds like more of an issue for animal control than the police." Sarah paused after her last statement and acted indifferent over the attack. "Is there anything else to know?"

"Not really. A couple of her neighbors called into the police station during the middle of the night. One of them reported a loud 'crashing sound' and the other said they heard a 'bear' growling. Dispatch requested that a unit come out to investigate, but it was a busy night so our guys weren't able to make it until early this morning." Harris turned and walked toward the kitchen. "One of the victim's friends showed up about an hour ago after seeing it on the news. She's outside with Officer Lindberg."

Sarah followed Harris to the heap of bones and flesh that used to be Emily. The gruesome scene didn't faze her, though she did recite a quick prayer for the victim in silence. Sarah's mother had been half Native-American and had taught her a few prayers during her childhood. Becoming numb to violence was part of being a police detective, but Sarah was determined not to forget her humanity.

"Her name's Emily Fisher." Harris said as they stood over the mutilated body. "She's been living here for about seven years, and she works…" he cleared his throat and corrected himself "worked as an office worker of some kind for the City."

Sarah nodded her head as she examined the wreckage that the beast had left behind. Emily's chest had been completely ripped open, the rib cage shattered, and the heart was missing. It was definitely Sarah's werewolf. She immediately wanted to go back outside and find Emily's friend in hopes of discovering a link between one of her suspects and Emily. However, first she needed to distract Harris. "Has animal control taken a look at this yet?"

"Oh yeah, they're here." He looked toward the back porch. "I think they're in the back yard right now. The zoo is sending over some kind of expert too. Do you want to talk to the guy?" Harris gave a hopeful look at Sarah that she would take over and let him get back to his Saturday ritual of drinking scotch and watching baseball.

"No thanks, Harris. I've actually got plans. Fun's all yours." Sarah was already half way to the front door before he could object. She heard him say something derogatory as she exited the house, but she didn't care. She was on a mission.

"Officer Lindberg," Sarah addressed Brad as she walked up to him. Brad was taking a statement from an older couple, but as soon as he heard Sarah call his name he turned his attention immediately to her. "I understand that one of the victim's friends is here?"

Brad's sapphire blue eyes made contact with Sarah's. By the way he was looking at her it was quite obvious that he was harboring some strong feelings for her. "Yes, Detective Chase. Her name is Ms. Keisha Williams. She's standing right over there." Brad motioned toward a young African-American woman, and then looked at Sarah like a puppy looking for his owner's approval.

"Thank you, Officer," Sarah replied. She could feel Brad's gaze as she walked away from him. Sarah knew he was interested in her, but she really wasn't sure she felt the same way; at least, not on a level that was more than sexual. Sarah knew there'd be a day when she had to start taking relationships seriously, but for now, she enjoyed her independence. Besides, it would take a pretty special guy to ever understand her 'other job'.

"Good afternoon, Ms. Williams," Sarah addressed Keisha. "I'm Detective Chase. I understand you were a friend of Emily Fisher's?"

"Yes," Keisha replied. "I gave a statement to that guy over there." Keisha pointed in the direction of Brad. "He asked me to stick around for you though." It was obvious that Keisha had been crying from the redness in her eyes, but she was mostly composed now as she spoke with Sarah.

"I appreciate you being so patient, Ms. Williams. This won't take long." Sarah pulled out her cell phone and turned on the voice recorder. "When was the last time you had contact with Emily Fisher?"

"Last night. We were downtown at Club 802 until about 1:30 AM. We both left from there in a taxi and I was dropped off first." Keisha fought back the return of her tears.

"Do you know if Emily tried to reach out to you or anyone else last night with regards to a wild animal or strange noises occurring around her house?" Sarah was doing her best to build her line of questioning so that the real question she wanted to ask wouldn't come out of left field.

"No. She didn't call or text me. I already talked with our other friends we were out with. Nothing."

"Okay, thank you, Ms. Williams." Sarah placed her cell phone back into her pocket, started to turn away and then paused. She drew in closer to Keisha and lowered her voice, so that no one else but Keisha could hear her next question. "You said you were at Club 802 last night, Ms. Williams?"

"Yes."

"I know this is a painful time for you...we're actually looking for a guy that might have been at that same club you were at last night." Sarah pulled her phone back out and showed Keisha the three pictures of her suspects. "I'm sorry for asking this, but did you see any of these men at the club last night?"

Keisha looked at the screen on Sarah's phone and immediately recognized one of them. "Yeah, I recognize that guy." She pointed to Stanley. "He was at the club last night. He even sat with us for a while." Keisha paused for a moment. "Stanley. His name was Stanley".

"Thank you, Ms. Williams. I really appreciate your help with that." Sarah knew she had her man. "I realize you've suffered a terrible loss and I promise we're going to do everything we can to catch the wild animal that attacked your friend."

Sarah headed back to her Camaro, slightly surprised that Keisha had identified Stanley Jones as the werewolf. He was some kind of a computer guy that worked for the Portland City Library, and there was definitely nothing intimidating about him on the outside. "Just goes to show you can't ever judge these bastards from their looks!" Sarah thought to herself. She cranked up the Def Leppard song that was playing on her stereo as she drove off in the direction of Stanley's neighborhood.

CHAPTER 5

It was a beautiful summer day at the park. Six-year old Sarah was wearing a pink dress and socks with matching ribbons in her hair. She swung to her heart's content on the playground as her mother walked toward her with two delicious ice cream cones in her hands. Sarah knew this was just a dream, but it was one of her most treasured memories of her mother and for a few moments she allowed herself to enjoy the fantasy.

Her mother's Native-American descent showed itself in her long, dark hair and brown eyes. She had a smile that radiated warmth and kindness, something that Sarah missed greatly when her mother left the following summer. She was only supposed to be gone for a few weeks, but those weeks quickly turned into months and eventually both Sarah and her step-father lost hope that her mother would ever return. After several years of infrequent letters and brief phone calls, Sarah and her step-father received word that her mother had passed away. It was the only wound that Sarah had never been able to fully recover from.

Sarah's dream turned gray as the clouds suddenly rushed in and covered the sun. The sky became dark and a chill instantly set upon the air. She stopped swinging and began shaking from fear when several black wolves appeared out of nowhere and surrounded her mother. Before Sarah could even let out a scream, three of the wolves leapt in the air and knocked her mother to the ground. Sarah looked away from the gruesome attack though she could still hear the terrible sounds of bones cracking and flesh being torn. After a few seconds, Sarah gathered enough courage to turn back around; the broken ice cream cones were all that remained where her mother had been.

The wolves then began encircling Sarah, snarling horribly and exposing their blood-stained teeth. She looked down for a brief moment and when she raised her head back up she was no longer a scared little girl, but rather a strong woman with an arsenal of weapons around her waist. Sarah shifted all of her weight back and swung herself through the air with Glocks in each hand firing at the wolves. She landed on the ground and turned just as one of the wolves lunged for her. Sarah raised her right hand in the wolf's direction but its jaws were only inches away from her face and she knew it was too late.

"Thunk." The sound of two car doors shutting at once woke Sarah abruptly from her dream. "Fucking werewolves!" She said to herself as she regained consciousness from her brief sleep. She sat up and watched as two figures dressed in all black, a man and a woman, walked toward Stanley's house. "Who the hell do you have visiting at this time of night, Stanley?" Sarah wondered out loud as she read 1:45 AM on her cell phone.

Stanley was already home when Sarah had arrived earlier in the day, and she knew it would have been suicide to attempt taking him out in his own domain. Werewolves were incredibly aware of their environments and pretty much impossible to sneak up on. Instead, she had decided to wait until Stanley came out of his house and hit him with a silver-tipped arrow while he was standing out in the open. Although it was a myth that silver actually killed werewolves, the precious metal was effective in slowing down their regeneration process.

The two figures rang the doorbell and a few seconds later Stanley's bedroom light turned on. Sarah pulled out her night vision goggles to get a better look at Stanley's "guests". The woman had long, dark brown hair, appeared to be in exceptional shape and was probably in her late 30's. The man, on the other hand, looked quite a bit younger, had a shaved head and was built like a professional football player. They were also both concealing firearms.

The woman rang the doorbell again and this time said something loud enough for Stanley to hear from inside his house, though Sarah couldn't make out the words. Thirty seconds later, another light turned on in Stanley's house and he opened the front door with a look of defeat. Sarah didn't observe any kind of angry scene although she could tell that Stanley was extremely uncomfortable in the presence of both his visitors. After the exchange of a few words Stanley slowly retreated back into his house while the other two followed him in. Sarah noticed that the man was carrying a small, metal briefcase.

"Great," Sarah said out loud, thinking that this new turn of events could make it extremely challenging to take Stanley down. She was guessing that the man and woman in black were either hunters like herself or worse, 'monsters'. The latter was something that Sarah had been preparing for, but thus far she had never taken on more than one beast at a time. While she waited for Stanley and his guests to make their next move, Sarah began constructing a plan of attack and thought back to her first werewolf kill.

It was six months after her initial altercation with a vampire that Sarah had been called out to investigate a case of arson at a local warehouse in downtown Portland. On her way back to her car, she'd caught a glimpse of something in the shadows following a young girl who had just walked out of an apartment complex. Back in those days Sarah didn't carry the arsenal she did now, so emptying two clips into the beast's skull while it swung wildly at her was the best she could do. A couple of bullets through one of the werewolf's eyes finally stunned it enough that Sarah was able to climb on its back and pry its head off with the survival knife she carried on her right thigh. A bit messy, but she had survived it all the same.

Fifteen minutes passed before Stanley and his two visitors walked out the front door of the house, with Stanley carrying a single suitcase and the man in black holding a small box with a few items spilling out of it. Stanley held his head low as he got into the backseat of the black Suburban parked in the driveway. The man in black placed Stanley's box in the rear of the vehicle and walked over to the passenger side, holding some kind of small device in his right hand. As the Suburban started up and pulled out into the street, there was a huge explosion and Stanley's house went up in flames.

"Guess that's what was in the briefcase," Sarah said to herself, waiting a few moments before she turned the key in her ignition. She followed the Suburban for several hours down I-5 south, making only one brief stop for gas. They crossed the California border shortly after sunrise and made their way through the Redwood forests and over to the old coastal highway.

Sarah was all too familiar with this part of northern California. Shortly after her mother's death, she and her step-father received an anonymous phone call letting them know that Alyssa Walker had passed away. A few days later, a box mysteriously showed up on their front door step with some of her mother's personal items and her ashes. Sarah and her step-father took a long road trip along the Oregon and California coast to spread her mother's ashes since she had always spoken fondly of the redwoods and the ocean.

After a few more hours of driving along the curvy coast highway, the fog became so thick that Sarah could no longer tell if the Suburban was still in front of her. She turned on her windshield wipers in an effort to improve her visibility when suddenly, a deer leapt out in front of her car. She tried to swerve around it, but her Camaro spun out of control and slammed into a tree several yards off the highway. Sarah slowly drifted out of consciousness as she watched the deer, unharmed, bound into the forest.

CHAPTER 6

"Ugh…" Sarah groaned as she leaned back from the steering wheel. She reached over to check her cell phone for service, but it was completely dead. With her head throbbing intensely, Sarah got out of the car and took inventory of her injuries, thankful that it was only her Camaro that appeared to be broken. She looked around for some kind of highway marker or sign, but the fog was still too dense to see anything. Having no idea what time it was or where she was now, Sarah began walking alongside the road, hoping to flag down a car for assistance.

As she walked down the lonely highway Sarah couldn't help but notice how creepy the surrounding forest seemed. There was an unnatural darkness that filled the spaces in between the trees and bushes, as though the shadow of a guardian spirit cloaked it from her peering eyes. A cold breeze permeated the air and made its way right through Sarah's black leather jacket, causing her to shiver almost uncontrollably. The summers were fairly warm in Portland so she wasn't exactly equipped for 45 degree weather.

On top of the cold temperature, Sarah began to feel light headed from what she guessed was a concussion. She looked down at her boots taking one step and then the next until she came across a gravel road off the highway. There were no exit signs or any other kind of signage to indicate where it might lead to. Sarah was concerned that she was going to soon pass out again so she decided to take her chances on the mysterious gravel road.

She could barely see ten feet in front of her as she made her way through the fog. The forest hugged each side of the narrow road tightly and Sarah began feeling like she was being watched from something behind the trees. Her thoughts turned to her nightmare about her mother and the wolves, prompting Sarah to remove her gun from its holster and hold it in her right hand. With the sunlight fading and the pain in her head getting worse, she was just about to turn around when she saw the outline of a large wooden sign up the road. Sarah moved closer toward the sign until she could read the letters: "Welcome to Hallows End".

"Thank God." She walked past the sign and headed down the road which had now turned from gravel to black cobblestone. The fog retreated enough that Sarah could see the road forking up ahead with what appeared to be the outline of some housing to the left and a modest downtown area to the right. Sarah preferred the thought of finding an open business with a phone rather than knocking on a bunch of strangers' doors so she headed to the right.

She slowly made her way past the dozen or so closed store fronts that occupied both sides of the street. The buildings were all Victorian style and were primarily comprised of either gray brick or stone. Large windows took up the majority of the store front space on the bottom floor, while it appeared that the top two stories of each building were dedicated to residences, though Sarah didn't see a single light on in any of the windows.

Along the side of the street there were several black metal lamp posts that stood about six feet high. Sarah observed that each of them contained intricate depictions of wolves, bats, gargoyles and other beasts. The entire scene made her feel like she was in a Stephen King novel.

Just past the downtown area, there was a large, two-story building on the left and a smaller one on her right with a 50's style sign on it that read "Dave's Diner". Sarah walked over to the diner hoping it might still be open on a Sunday evening, but the door was locked and there were no lights on inside.

"Can I help you, dear?" a voice asked from behind. Sarah nearly jumped out of her skin as she swung around to see an elderly woman in her 80's standing on the sidewalk.

"Yes!" Sarah said as she laughed at herself for having been startled. "I'm afraid my car went off the road several miles back. May I please use your phone?" She raised her cell phone in the air for the woman to see. "I'm afraid mine is dead."

"I'm so sorry," the woman responded sympathetically. "My phone is only an internal line to reach those living in Hallows End. There are a few homes and businesses with lines that reach outside of our town, but everyone retires rather early on Sundays." The woman took a couple of steps toward Sarah and gently placed one of her hands on Sarah's arm. "My name is Rosemary, dear. Why don't you stay in my guest room tonight?"

"That's very kind of you, Rosemary," Sarah said with a slight trace of frustration in her voice, "but are you sure there's no one awake whose phone I could use? Surely someone has a cell phone? You see, I'm a police detective and..."

"I'm afraid cell phones don't work in Hallows End," Rosemary interrupted. "Tell you what; why don't you stay at my house tonight, get yourself some rest, and you can use the phone at the diner first thing tomorrow morning."

Sarah knew from experience that trying to argue with someone Rosemary's age was pointless. Besides, her head was pounding, and at this point she knew that getting some sleep was probably more important than making a phone call. Sarah reluctantly accepted Rosemary's offer and followed her back to her house which was located just down the street from the diner.

"Thank you for your help, Rosemary," Sarah said as they walked slowly along the sidewalk. The sidewalk bore the same black and gray colored stones as the main street, though they were smaller in size. Sarah had become so dizzy that it was taking all of her concentration just to stay upright and not trip on the small crevasses between the cobble stone. "By the way; my name is Sarah."

"It's lovely to meet you, Sarah," Rosemary replied as they walked up the steps to the house. The moment Sarah entered the home she was met with the sweet aroma of vanilla and cinnamon. There was a fireplace radiating heat from the living room straight ahead and a small set of carpeted stairs to the left.

"You must be exhausted, my dear," Rosemary said softly as she took Sarah's jacket and hung it by the door next to her own red coat. "Can I get you anything to eat or perhaps I could make you some tea?"

"No thank you," Sarah answered, doing her best not to collapse right there on the hard wood floor of the entryway. "A bed, however, would be very much appreciated."

"Of course." Rosemary smiled as she led Sarah up the stairs to the guest room. The room was decorated in soft tones of blue and yellow with a mural of white horses running in a meadow with a magnificent mountain range in the distance.

"Please let me know if there's anything I can get for you." She smiled and closed the door to the room behind her. Sarah let out a sigh of exhaustion as she threw her boots and jeans into a heap on the floor and quickly went to sleep.

Rosemary made her way back downstairs and set a kettle on the stove for tea. She went over to the kitchen phone and dialed a single number.

"Good evening, Rosemary," a deep and pleasant sounding voice said on the other end of the line.

"Good evening Dr. Nemitz. I just wanted to let you know that we have a visitor. A young woman named Sarah. She says she's a police officer."

"Ah, yes. It's okay, Rosemary," Dr. Nemitz said in a soothing tone. "I've been expecting her. Please see to it that she has a good night's rest and I'll come over in the morning to introduce myself." Rosemary assured him that she would take good care of Sarah and wished the doctor a good night.

Dr. Nemitz hung up the phone, sat back in his reading chair and smiled. He was in his late 70's, and had an air of wisdom about him that made him appear almost god-like. His white hair and beard were perfectly combed, and his pale blue eyes were lit with a subtle intensity. He looked toward the corner of the room where a figure in the shadows stood. "She's here," he said.

The figure moved toward Dr. Nemitz slightly, allowing the light in the dimly lit room to reveal a beautiful blonde woman in her early 20's. With tears forming in her eyes, the young woman looked at him. "Finally," she said. "I shall meet my sister."

CHAPTER 7

Sarah slowly opened her eyes and looked at the clock: 6:15 AM. She groaned, forcing herself to roll out of bed, and made her way to the bathroom for a quick shower. Her head was still aching from the accident and, unfortunately, she hadn't slept very well due to the noise coming from downtown all night. Evidently, Hallows End had quite the night life, which Sarah found odd. The town had appeared completely dead earlier that evening and Rosemary even mentioned that the people here retire early.

Warm water streaming from the shower head provided some much needed relief from her pounding head and sore muscles. The previous day's events were a blur thanks to the concussion she had incurred during the accident. Sarah knew her first priority should be getting her car taken care of and returning to Portland, but she wasn't ready to give up on Stanley's trail quite yet. Besides, she had plenty of vacation time to use.

She made her way down the stairs, eager to use a phone so she could let Chief Reynolds know about her impromptu vacation. The Chief wouldn't be happy, but he'd get over it. Sarah saw Rosemary and an older gentleman sitting at the kitchen table drinking coffee. Rosemary looked up and greeted her with a warm smile. "Good morning, Ms. Chase."

Sarah's eyes widened. She didn't remember telling Rosemary her last name. "Good morning, Rosemary."

"Sarah, isn't it?" asked the older gentleman in a thick Austrian accent. "My name is Dr. Albert Nemitz." He stood up and extended his hand out to Sarah. He was a tall man, over six feet, and wore a dark red cardigan over a white dress shirt with gray slacks. His white beard reminded Sarah of her grandfather Chase.

"Please, join us." He motioned for her to have a seat with them at the table. "Rosemary called me first thing this morning to tell me about your predicament. I want to assure you that I've already taken care of everything." Dr. Nemitz paused to take a sip of his coffee while Rosemary brought over a fresh cup for Sarah.

"I'm afraid we don't have a mechanic in our town," Dr. Nemitz continued, "so I had your car towed to the next closest one. It's about twenty miles from here. They told me your car should be fixed by Wednesday."

Sarah was relieved to know her Camaro was able to be repaired. However, she was also frustrated over being stuck in Hallows End. Unless the black Suburban had ended up in Hallows End as well, Stanley's trail was going to be cold by the time she got her car back.

"Thanks for taking care of that for me, Dr. Nemitz," Sarah said as she took a drink of her coffee. "Rosemary, you mentioned that the Diner had a phone. Do you think the owner would mind if I called my Chief to let him know that I'm all right?"

"You needn't worry about that either, Ms. Chase," Dr. Nemitz interjected. "I already spoke to him." Dr. Nemitz appeared quite proud of himself as he took another drink of his coffee. "I explained to Chief Reynolds that you were in a minor car accident last night, told him you were fine, and that we would get you back to Portland as soon as possible." Sarah was speechless and now completely on edge over how Dr. Nemitz knew who she worked for.

"I'm sorry," Rosemary chimed in, seeing Sarah's look of confusion. She reached over and patted the back of Sarah's hand. "I went back into your room after you fell asleep and found the information on your driver's license and badge. You said you were a police officer, but I had to make sure, since you were carrying a gun."

"Please understand, Ms. Chase," Dr. Nemitz interposed, "We don't get a lot of visitors in Hallows End, especially armed ones. We had to make sure you weren't a danger to the townsfolk." Sarah stared into Dr. Nemitz eyes for a reading on whether she could trust him, but also admitted inwardly that his and Rosemary's actions did make sense.

Dr. Nemitz saw that she was feeling uncomfortable. "Please accept my apology, Sarah. I shouldn't have taken it upon myself to contact your employer. Why don't we head over to the diner and you can call him yourself. I insist you allow me to buy you breakfast to make up for my over-zealousness."

"Okay." Sarah wanted to confirm that Dr. Nemitz had truly called Chief Reynolds; though she couldn't imagine what the doctor's motives would be for lying to her about it.

"Ah, very good then," he said happily. After they finished their coffee, Dr. Nemitz and Sarah left for the diner. As they stepped outside, Sarah took in the smell of the ocean close by. The sun's warmth shone down on her face. She held a great fondness for ocean, and on the rare occasion she took a vacation day, that's where she spent it.

"The town does grow on you," Dr. Nemitz said as they made their way down the street. "I founded Hallows End in the spring of 1929, right before the Great Depression." Sarah looked at him in disbelief since that would make him over 100 years old. "I know what you're thinking." He laughed and turned to look at her. "Age has been good to me; lots of vitamins."

Sarah didn't believe for a second that Dr. Nemitz was really that old, but she refrained from pressing him on the subject. Once they arrived at the diner he insisted on opening the door for her, saying "Regardless of current trends, a gentleman should always demonstrate good manners". Sarah was amused as she wasn't really the type to let a guy open a door for her, but she played along to appease him. After all, he was 100 years old.

The sound of the Big Bopper's "Helllooo Baaaby" line filled the entry way as Sarah walked through the door of the diner. "Clever," she thought to herself, hearing the door chime repeat upon Dr. Nemitz's walking in. The restaurant was decorated in a 50's style theme with red vinyl furnishings and black and white floor tiles. There was a jukebox in the corner playing an Elvis Presley song. Her step father used to listen to Elvis while cooking breakfast on Sunday mornings. It had been one of the few rituals he continued after Sarah's mother had left.

"Good morning, Dr. Nemitz."

A tall, black man walked toward them. He was thin, probably in his late 40's and wore a smile from ear to ear. He had a collared white shirt on under a full length apron that read 'Dave's Diner'. "Who's your guest this morning?" He bowed slightly to Sarah.

"Hi," Sarah said, quickly returning from her trip down memory lane. "I'm Detective Sarah Chase."

"Welcome to Dave's Diner, Detective Chase; I'm David." he replied, still grinning like today was the happiest day of his life. He showed them to a booth, then went behind the counter to grab a coffee pot. "So Detective, what brings you to Hallows End?"

"You can call me Sarah," she replied. "My car went off the road last night. There was a lot of fog, deer jumped out in front of me…I'm sure you guys get one like me every now and then with a similar story, right?"

"Oh, sure," David responded, returning to the booth and pouring coffee.

"A little quiet, isn't it?" Sarah asked, looking around the empty restaurant.

"Yes, well, as I'm sure you probably heard last night, Hallows End is full of night owls." David laughed. "There's still a few of us though who wake up with the sun, isn't that right, Dr. Nemitz?"

"Indeed," Dr. Nemitz responded raising his cup in agreement. David took their breakfast orders and disappeared into the kitchen. Just as he left their booth, the greeting at the entrance was heard again and a tall, attractive woman with long black hair walked in. She wore a sheriff's uniform, and appeared to be on a mission as she marched up to the counter.

"Hey, Dave! Breakfast to go, please," she shouted. David gave a friendly shout back from the kitchen. She stepped behind the counter and poured herself some coffee.

"Diana," Dr. Nemitz said, waving her over to their booth. "Please, come meet my guest. This is Sarah Chase, the police detective from Portland." As Diana walked over, Sarah noticed that Dr. Nemitz appeared to be quite taken with the sheriff.

"Pleasure to meet you, Ms. Chase," Diana said warmly. "Dr. Nemitz told me about your accident last night. I hope you're feeling all right this morning?"

"My head's a little foggy," Sara responded, "but I'll be fine. Any chance that someone in Hallows End owns a black Suburban?"

"No," Diana replied. "There are only three cars in the entire town. My car, Dr. Nemitz' Cadillac, and a small pick-up that the townsfolk use for various errands."

"I was tracking a black Suburban last night when my car went off the road." She felt comfortable bringing the topic up since Diana was a fellow law enforcement agent. "A man in that car is a suspect in a case I'm handling."

"I can run the plates for you?" Diana offered. She pulled out a small notebook from her shirt pocket and handed it to Sarah.

"I'd appreciate that." She wrote down the license plate information and handed the pad back to Diana. She couldn't help but notice the sheriff's arm muscles were rippling below the short sleeves of her uniform. "So, it sounds like I'm going to be here a couple of days while my car's getting fixed. I take it you have a gym in your town?"

Diana grinned proudly. "We certainly do. If you head over there today, tell Martin I sent you and he'll take care of you. Just don't fall for any of his cheesy pick-up lines."

"Ah, yes," Dr. Nemitz interjected with a roll of his eyes, "Martin is quite a player." Sarah almost laughed out loud at the doctor's use of the word 'player'. "Before you head over there though," he continued, "I've arranged for you to visit the Candy Shoppe after breakfast. Tremissa is the manager over there and will help you with clothing or anything else you might need during your stay. I must warn you though that her tastes in decorating are a bit extreme. Truth is I order most of my things through the internet."

"Okay," Sarah said, thinking about how different the hospitality was in Hallows End from Portland. Diana excused herself when David called her order up, and as she exited the diner, a young man entered and sat down at the counter. He was probably in his late-20's, Sarah guessed, with a thin build and wavy blonde hair.

Dr. Nemitz noticed where Sarah's attention had wandered to. "His name is Clive," he said with a grin. "He's a good looking young man, isn't he?"

Sarah blushed slightly and quickly turned her head back toward the doctor. "Dr. Nemitz, do you know if any of the towns nearby have rental cars?" she asked, trying to change the topic of conversation from Clive.

"They might," Dr. Nemitz replied with a slight nod of his head. "In a hurry to leave Hallows End already?" he asked teasingly.

"Possibly." Sarah found herself pulling back now that Diana had left their company. While Dr. Nemitz had been obvious in his attempt to win Sarah over, her instincts told her that the good doctor wasn't to be completely trusted.

"Breakfast is served," David announced as he placed two impressive looking plates of eggs, turkey bacon and fresh fruit on the table. Sarah was thankful for David interrupting the awkward moment that had followed her last response.

While they ate, Dr. Nemitz told Sarah about his leaving Austria shortly after World War I and his travels to California. However, she was only half invested in the conversation as she was distracted with frustration over her accident and losing the black Suburban in the fog. "If only that damned deer hadn't jumped out in front of me," she thought to herself.

After they had finished breakfast, Dr. Nemitz arranged for Sarah to use the phone in David's office near the back of the diner. She wasn't looking forward to her conversation with Chief Reynolds and was actually thankful that Dr. Nemitz had called him earlier in the morning. She hoped the news of her accident would buy her a little sympathy.

As they approached the door to David's office Dr. Nemitz turned to Sarah. "I have a rather busy day today, but I'd love it if you could join me for dinner tonight; say, 6 o'clock?"

Sarah wasn't excited about the idea, but she couldn't come up with a solid reason to refuse his offer either. "Sure."

"Fantastic! I have a bottle of Pinot from your neck of the woods, and I've been looking forward to sharing it with someone who'd actually appreciate it." Sarah nodded her head in enthusiasm, although in truth, she hardly ever drank wine. "Until tonight then." He opened the door for Sarah and then closed it behind her.

Dr. Nemitz made his way back to the main dining area and headed over to the counter where Clive was.

"I wonder if you would do me a favor." He placed his hand on Clive's shoulder. "The woman you saw me with is a very special guest of Hallows End. Do you think you could make it a point today to ensure that she receives our town's finest hospitality?" Dr. Nemitz looked directly into Clive's silver blue eyes to convey how important the task was that was being asked of him.

"Of course, Dr. Nemitz." Clive had lived in Hallows End nearly all his life and looked up to Dr. Nemitz as a father figure. There wasn't anything the doctor could ask of him that he wouldn't do. "If you don't mind me asking, who is she?"

"She is the daughter of Alyssa Walker."

"Does she know about us?" Clive asked nervously.

"No," Dr. Nemitz said as he walked toward the exit. "Please look after her, Clive, and make sure none of our more rowdy residents give her a hard time. It's not often that we have a stranger staying in our town and I don't want anyone scaring her off."

CHAPTER 8

Sarah wasn't feeling great about having lied to Chief Reynolds as to why she was stranded on the coast of northern California. Telling him the truth wasn't an option, so instead Sarah told him that she'd decided to visit the spot where she and her step father had spread her mother's ashes. She hated using the 'mom card', but it had worked. She was now officially on vacation for the rest of the week.

During her short walk over to the Candy Shoppe, Sarah gazed upon the unique downtown area of Hallows End which was much easier to appreciate in the daylight. Although the architectural style was reminiscent of 19th century England, it also felt somewhat modern because everything was in such pristine condition and appeared as if it had just been built yesterday.

"Hi ya, Sexy," were the first words that greeted Sarah as she walked into the Candy Shoppe. Her eyes grew wide, searching for the source of the voice.

HALLOWS END

The store looked like a cross between a very trendy clothing boutique and some perverse, Tim Burton nightmare. Anatomically correct mannequins (both male and female) stood amongst the clothing and shoe racks sporting bondage gear, holding adult magazines in their hands and wearing running shoes on their feet. An impressive array of Marilyn Monroe collectibles was displayed next to a shelf of body oils and lubricants. There were also classic 40's and 50's movie posters framed on every wall, along with a sex swing suspended from the ceiling that had various styles of socks hanging on it.

"Find anything you like?" said the elusive voice. Sarah turned around to see a petite woman in her early 20's sporting a very short skirt, grey sweater and pink dyed hair. The girl looked like the sexual fantasy of teenage boys who read too many comic books. "Is there anything you wanna try on?" she asked, "...or try out?" she added with an impish grin.

"Um," Sarah was feeling incredibly awkward. "I just need some clothes for the next couple of days and a pair of tennis shoes." Sarah was hardly a prude when it came to her sexuality, but she also wasn't the type to flirt or tease with another woman.

"Yeah, I was just messing with you." The girl winked at Sarah. "My name's Tremissa. Dr. Nemitz told me you'd be coming by." Tremissa looked Sarah up and down once and then headed off toward the shelves, grabbing several items.

"You've got a unique taste for décor," Sarah said as she tried to follow Tremissa around the aisles of clothing, collectibles and adult toys.

"Yeah, the place had no flavor until I took it over. Not everyone in this town is willing to admit they like it, but trust me, they do." Tremissa turned toward Sarah and dumped a stack of clothes, a pair of black tennis shoes and a neon pink vibrator into Sarah's arms. "Here. No need to try anything on; this will all fit you perfectly and should last you a few days while you're in town."

Sarah was surprised as she glanced over the pile and admitted to herself that it all looked like clothing she would actually wear. "This looks great…but I don't really need this." Her arms were full so she simply pointed her nose at the vibrator lying on top of the pile.

"Oh, you probably do need it around here," Tremissa responded sarcastically, "but if you don't want it." Tremissa removed the vibrator from the pile and proceeded to tell Sarah that Dr. Nemitz had insisted he would pay for everything. Sarah walked over to the sales counter while Tremissa began placing the clothing in two large, bright pink shopping bags.

"How long have you lived in Hallows End?" Sarah asked, attempting to make small talk and hoping that Tremissa wasn't going to offer her any more 'toys'.

"Pretty long time now. I know what you're thinking: girl like me in a town like this." Tremissa rolled her eyes upward and bobbed her head side to side. "You'd be surprised though. Hallows End can be quite the party town as I'm sure you heard last night."

"I did notice that." Sarah thought back to the loud music and howls of laughter that she heard coming from downtown all night. She wasn't naïve, and while she was accepting of Rosemary and Dr. Nemitz' assistance, she knew something didn't feel right about Hallows End.

Tremissa handed Sarah the two bags of clothes as she smacked her bubble gum. "You're going to the spa later, right?" she asked.

"Is that what they call the gym here?" Sarah asked.

"Yeah," Tremissa said with another roll of her eyes. "Make sure you talk to Martin while you're there." Tremissa leaned over the sales counter slightly. "Tell him you're looking for something." Tremissa's last words rolled off her tongue like a snake spewing strawberry-flavored venom.

"Excuse me?" Sarah pretended not to have understood the meaning behind Tremissa's words.

"Honey, no one ends up in Hallows End unless they're looking for something," Tremissa said accusingly as she backed off the counter. "Or someone."

"Sounds like maybe I should be talking to you?" Sarah said with an edge in her voice. Tremissa's 'alterna-girl' act and bubble gum smacking were getting on her nerves.

"Sorry," Tremissa said, shrugging her shoulders. She tilted her head to the right and then popped a large bubble with her gum. "Don't know anything."

Sarah knew Tremissa was messing with her. She stared into Tremissa's eyes, trying to read her for clues. Several seconds passed by with neither woman saying a word.

"Just so you know, I'm a bisexual nymphomaniac," Tremissa stated, breaking the silence, "so if we stand here eye-fucking each other for much longer I'm gonna want more." Tremissa crossed her arms and continued to stare back at Sarah.

Sarah shook her head and turned toward the exit. "Thanks for the clothes," she said from the sidewalk, letting the door close behind her.

Clearly, Tremissa wasn't going to be of any help, but at least Sarah had a lead. She looked down the street at the "Spa" located across from the diner. Sarah considered going directly there to find out what this guy Martin knew, but instead she turned left toward the rest of the small downtown area. The Sheriff's station had to be fairly close and before Sarah started stirring things up in Hallows End, she wanted to find out if Diana was going to be an ally…or an enemy.

CHAPTER 9

As Sarah made her way past the short row of store fronts, she noticed that, unlike the Candy Shoppe, the rest of the businesses in Hallows End seemed quite typical. There was a florist's shop, a small café, a hardware store and several professional services that included an attorney's office and an accounting firm. Past downtown and located closer to the entrance of the town stood the Sheriff's station. It was a small, one story building and was much plainer looking than those in the downtown area.

Before she stepped inside, Sarah looked around to get a sense of her surroundings. She didn't feel like she was necessarily in danger, but Sarah wasn't the type to ever be caught unprepared. There was only one road leading in to Hallows End. It forked at what appeared to be a large park set in the middle of the town. To the right, the cobblestone street headed toward the downtown area with the Sheriff's office being the first building on the inside of the street near the park. Unlike the previous night when the fog and fading sunlight had impaired her view, Sarah could clearly see a series of residential homes to the left of the divide.

"Good morning again, Ms. Chase," Diana said as Sarah walked into the Sheriff's station. The building looked even smaller inside, with a small waiting area in the front and an office surrounded by glass to the left. Diana was sitting in the glass office with a cup of coffee in her hand. "Come on in." She motioned Sarah in with a nod of her head.

"I ran those plates you asked me about. They're fakes." She handed a single page document to Sarah. "Those plates aren't issued to anyone in the state of Oregon." Sarah wasn't really surprised by the news, though she was disappointed.

"Any chance the Suburban could have ended up in Hallows End?" Sarah asked as she sat down in front of Diana's desk.

"Not likely. Granted, I was on call last night so I wouldn't have seen it come through town myself. However, chances are pretty good that if there was a black Suburban roaming around Hallows End, one of the residents would have reported it to me. We don't get a lot of visitors here, so I get called pretty much any time that something slightly 'out of the norm' comes up."

Sarah couldn't tell yet if Diana knew more than she was letting on, so she decided to push a little harder. "Do you mind if I ask around a bit?"

"Not at all," Diana replied with an amused grin. "Just don't take it personally if people are a little stand-offish. Like I said, they're not used to many visitors; especially police detectives from the city." Sarah was surprised that Diana wasn't more threatened by her request. Her experience with small-town sheriffs in the past had been that they were usually much more territorial.

"How long have you been the Sheriff in Hallows End?" Sarah hoped that by engaging Diana in some small talk she could determine whether or not she could be trusted.

"A long time now." Diana's eyes wandered upward in thought. "In fact, I can barely remember what my life was like before I came to Hallows End."

"So, you must really like it here?"

"Well, it's definitely home," Diana said leaning back in her chair. "When you've been around as long as I have, peace and quiet from the masses tends to be more important than a good night life," she chuckled.

Sarah couldn't help but look at Diana like she was crazy. The sheriff was, at most, in her mid 40's, and was talking as if she were twice that age. The thought did enter Sarah's mind that Dr. Nemitz and Diana could be vampires, but they didn't fit the mold. Both of them were obviously morning people (which vampires were not) and neither had looked at Sarah like she was 'on the menu' (something vampires struggle with when looking at a human). Admittedly, Sarah had only encountered a handful of vampires in her life, but she still felt confident that neither the doctor nor the Sheriff was the 'blood-sucking' type…nor did Sarah believe they were werewolves.

"Judging by the noise coming from downtown last night, I'd say Hallows End has a pretty good night life," Sarah countered with a smile.

"Ah yes, that. One of our residents owns a night club downtown called Lucifer's Garden. She has a few members of this town convinced that acting like a bunch of wild teenagers in the middle of the night is a great way to overcome their boredom with our 'small town' lifestyle."

"Why does she stay in Hallows End?

"The owner of the night club also happens to be Dr. Nemitz' daughter. Hallows End is kind of a 'family affair'. So even though Elise, his daughter, rebels against the lifestyle and traditions of our small town, she has no desire to leave. In fact, over the years, she's managed to recruit quite a few new friends to move here."

Sarah didn't completely understand the situation, but her morning was starting to disappear. Since Diana had given her 'blessing' to ask around, Sarah planned to head right over to the Spa and talk to Martin.

"Well, I've taken up enough of your time, Sheriff." Sarah stood up to shake Diana's hand. "Thank you so much for your help."

"Ms. Chase," Diana said as Sarah began to leave her office. "I know you're from the city and from what I can tell, you seem like a pretty intelligent detective. Just, please know that most of the residents here are good souls. And, if you do find something...I'm here to help."

Sarah nodded and left. She wasn't exactly sure what Diana meant, but as she walked out on to the sidewalk and headed for the Spa all doubt left her mind. Sarah knew her arriving in Hallows End was no coincidence. Stanley Jones was hiding here and Sarah was going to find him!

CHAPTER 10

On her way to the spa, Sarah ran through different scenarios in her head for what links might exist between Stanley, the two individuals in the black Suburban and Hallows End. She didn't get the impression that Diana was trying to protect Stanley, but she guessed that someone else might be. Perhaps Dr. Nemitz was behind the mystery although Sarah couldn't figure out why he would invite her to stay in town if he wanted to protect Stanley from her.

The Spa was located at the very end of the downtown area across from Dave's Diner. As soon as Sarah stepped inside she knew why the residents called it a 'spa', and not just a gym. The lobby floor and counters were all dark marble and granite, giving it the look of a five-star hotel rather than a small town health club. There were also magnificent, life-size statues made of charcoal-gray steel that represented the mythological gods of Greece, Rome and other various cultures.

"You must be Sarah!" A young, blonde girl appeared from behind the service counter. "My name is Brittany," she said in a sugary sweet, valley girl voice as she placed her hand on her chest. Sarah raised her right eyebrow and was surprised Brittany didn't have to look down at her own name tag to remember it. She was sporting a form-fitting t-shirt that read "We'll Make You Sweat" and her hair was braided in an "I Dream of Genie" style.

"Dr. Nemitz already took care of everything. Whatever you'd like to do today is on the house. We have a cardio theatre, a swimming pool, kickboxing studio, free weights, a sauna, tanning beds, manicurist, hair stylist and a masseuse who's available by appointment." Brittany stood there with a huge smile on her face as though she were proud that she had remembered all of her lines.

"Thank you, Brittany," Sarah responded with as sweet a tone as she could muster. Brittany was clearly a few cookies short of a full jar, but Sarah could tell that she meant well. "Is Martin around by any chance?"

"He's in a personal training session right now, but if you'd like to start your workout I'll have him come find you the moment he's done. It will probably be about an hour or so."

"That would be great. Thanks." Brittany handed her a locker room key and just as Sarah turned away from the counter, she bumped right into Clive from the diner.

"Oh, I'm sorry," Clive said as their bodies briefly collided into one another's. A powerful vibe of sexual radiance surged throughout Sarah's entire body. Sarah was the first to admit she tended to like younger guys. They typically kept themselves in better shape and weren't often looking for commitment, something that Sarah was determined to avoid at this stage in her life.

"No, no, it was me," Sarah said smiling. "I don't know where I'm going today."

"Well, that's understandable since you're new in town," Clive responded with a flirtatious grin. Sarah was suddenly self-conscious about carrying a large, pink shopping bag in each hand. Pink wasn't a color she chose to wear or accessorize with often. It was too 'girly' for her.

"My name is Clive, by the way," he said rather shyly as he ran his right hand through his wavy, blonde hair. "I saw you at the diner earlier and wanted to introduce myself, but you looked like you were talking over important stuff with the doc."

"Nice to meet you, Clive. My name is Sarah." She couldn't help but notice out of the corner of her eye that Brittany was watching them as if they were in a cheesy scene from some Nicholas Sparks movie. Clive stood there smiling at Sarah for just a second too long as there was now an awkward silence occurring between them. "I'm gonna go work out now. Bye, Clive."

Half way to the locker room Sarah heard Clive shout across the lobby, "Maybe we'll bump into each other 'again. It's a small town after all." Sarah almost laughed at Clive's attempt at a pick-up line. Still, she had to admit she might not mind bumping into Clive again.

Sarah attempted her usual workout routine; however, the after effects of her concussion impacted her intensity level. On more than one occasion, she snuck a peek at Clive's slender and toned body. She never looked long enough for him to catch her, although she did notice him admiring her.

She discovered a small kickboxing studio off the main weight room floor, and was about half way into her kickboxing drills when a Hispanic gentleman entered the room.

"Ms. Chase? My name is Martin. Brittany said that you asked for me?" Sarah stopped hitting the bag and turned toward him. He was a good looking guy; short and well-built with an extensive number of tattoos on his neck and arms.

"Hello, Martin," Sarah said, keeping her tone neutral. "I had an interesting conversation with Tremissa over at the Candy Shoppe earlier. She thought maybe you could help me find something?" Sarah grabbed her towel and wiped the sweat from her forehead.

"You're a cop, aren't you?" Martin asked with a cocky half-grin. Sarah was a little surprised that he had pegged her so quickly. "Trust me, I've had my share of run-ins; I know a cop when I see one. So," he paused momentarily, "who are you looking for?"

"I was tracking a murder suspect last night when my car slid off the road in the fog. The guy was riding in a black Suburban with tinted windows and fake Oregon license plates."

"Black Suburban, huh?" Martin repeated as his eyes momentarily shifted away from her. Sarah could tell by his delay that he was about to give her a bullshit answer. "Afraid there's only a couple of cars in this town and a black Suburban ain't one of them. Sorry."

Sarah knew Martin had information, but he was clearly attached to someone's leash; probably the same individual who was pulling Tremissa's strings.

"Well, I guess Tremissa was wrong then." Sarah turned back to beating the crap out of the black leather bag. She wasn't actually done talking to Martin, but she figured blowing him off would get under his skin; hopefully enough that he would give her something useful.

"Tell you what," Martin said, raising his voice so that Sarah could hear him over her grunts and kicks. "There is someone who might be able to help you out." Sarah immediately stopped and turned back toward him.

"Her name is Elise. She operates Lucifer's Garden, the night club downtown. Why don't you drop by tonight around ten and I'll introduce you."

Sarah found it interesting that Martin was now talking about the same person whom Diana had told her was behind the late night scene in Hallows End. Perhaps

Elise was secretly using the town as a hiding place for werewolves and vampires. It would certainly explain the rowdy nightlife, although Sarah didn't want to assume too much before actually meeting Elise.

"No need for introductions, Martin. I appreciate the information. I'll just go by and see her after my workout."

"Heh, sure you will," Martin half-laughed, "I realize patience isn't a virtue among detectives, but I'm afraid you're going to have to find something else to do with your day, Ms. Chase. Elise is a total night owl. She won't even be around the club until a few minutes before it opens."

"Fine," Sarah said, annoyed as she turned away to finish her workout. "Guess I'll just have to find something to keep myself busy until tonight then." She emphasized her words with a roundhouse kick that sent a resounding 'thud' through the entire studio.

"Okay....see you around 10," Martin said, taking his cue to leave Sarah alone to her workout. On his way back to the lobby, he shouted a "hey" in Clive's direction. Thanks to Martin having left the studio door open during his conversation with Sarah, Clive had heard everything.

Meanwhile, Sarah finished her workout so vigorously that her dizziness returned from the night before, and she almost passed out. A night club owner who wasn't available during the day and hosted wild parties in the middle of the night screamed 'vampire' in

Sarah's mind. Even worse, it sounded like this Elise character had friends, one of which could very well be Stanley. Sarah wasn't equipped to take on an army of 'monsters'. "Dammit!" she screamed out loud with her final punch of the bag.

CHAPTER 11

It was well past noon by the time Sarah had finished her workout and showered. She stepped outside of the Spa and paused, unsure what her next move should be. Diana had given her permission to ask around town, but surely the sheriff knew that vampires and werewolves were lurking everywhere. Sarah took a mental inventory of the weapons she had: a gun with three clips of silver bullets, a survival knife with a silver plated blade and a small, ultra-powerful flashlight. The flashlight couldn't kill a monster, but it could most certainly blind one long enough to give Sarah a couple seconds advantage during an attack.

"Hey, Sarah, wait up." Her train of thought was broken as she turned around to see Clive running to catch up with her.

"Does Hallows End assign a stalker to all of its guests?" Sarah quipped with a half-smile.

"Just the pretty ones," Clive retorted with a bashful grin. "How would you like your own personal tour guide to Hallows End for the day? I'll show you around, we'll get some lunch?"

Sarah wasn't really looking to have a puppy dog at her heels while she was trying to discover Stanley's whereabouts, but she also considered that the townspeople might be more open with her if Clive was by her side. "Sure. I've just got to drop this stuff back off at my room and then you can show me around."

Clive and Sarah spent the afternoon visiting every store in Hallows End. Sarah found the residents to be friendly, but no one would admit they had any knowledge of a black Suburban. Unlike Tremissa and Martin, however, the rest of the residents didn't toy with Sarah as much as just side-step her questions. None of them appeared to be of the vampire or werewolf kind either, though Sarah was beginning to doubt whether or not she was really that much of an expert on the matter. After all, of the three suspects, Stanley had been the least likely by Sarah's estimates to be a werewolf.

"What do you think of the town?" Clive asked as they walked away from the downtown area toward the park. Sarah wanted to see the rest of Hallows End so she could complete the mental map in her head.

"Everyone seems really nice. Is there anywhere else people go around here outside of downtown?" While it was obvious that Clive wasn't going to be able to help her with the investigation, she did find herself enjoying his company. He was the only person in town who didn't appear to be hiding something from her, although she had considered that perhaps he was just better at lying than the rest of them.

"Well, there's the library. It's on the way to Dr. Nemitz' house, but the guy who oversees it, Tom, he doesn't work on Mondays. Tomorrow would be a better day to go there." Clive walked next to Sarah with both hands inside of his jeans pockets, like an unsure teenager trying to decide when to make a move. "Outside of that most of us just kind of do our own thing, whether it's going down to the beach, walking in the park, tending our gardens."

"Tending your gardens, huh?" Sarah laughed.

Clive smiled. "Yeah, I know it probably sounds funny, but everyone who lives in Hallows End contributes in some way to the community. Those like me who choose to live in houses all contribute by growing fruits and vegetables, raising small livestock, etc. The ones who live in the apartments run the store fronts downtown as their way of contributing." Clive's voice drifted out as he noticed Sarah had stopped paying attention to him. She was instead looking around in awe at the extraordinary display of marble statues in the park.

"This is the Garden of Spirits," Clive explained. "When a resident of Hallows End passes, we honor them by placing a statue here with their name etched in the stone. The statues resemble creatures of both legend and the modern world. There's no church or organized religion in Hallows End, so people who want to practice their spiritual beliefs usually come here."

Sarah knelt down in front of a statue of a large wolf and read the name, "William Luse". Clive moved next to Sarah and lightly passed his hand over the etched marble. "William was Tom's, our Librarian's, older brother. His statue represents the mighty wolf Amarok who was born of Native-American legend. William was a very strong man who protected those who were unable to protect themselves."

Sarah assumed by the tone of Clive's voice that William must have served in the military. She stood back up and continued to walk around admiring the statues. "Dr. Nemitz mentioned that Hallows End has been around for over 80 years, yet there's only, what, like 20 or 30 statues here? Is this everyone from Hallows End who's died?" Clive got an odd look on his face and looked down.

"It's complicated. Not every man and woman who's died in Hallows End has a statue. In our town, you must die honorably in order to be honored." Clive's voice seemed to trail off at the end of his sentence. He suddenly appeared very nervous as Sarah made her way toward the back row of statues. He caught up with her at once and reached for her hand.

"I hope you don't mind, Sarah, but…" Clive leaned in and kissed her. Sarah had heard the expression 'swept off one's feet', but she had never experienced it for herself until that moment. It was as though her entire spirit broke away from the constricting scars of her life, allowing her to enjoy only the simple pleasure of embracing. There was something intoxicating in the air; perhaps a scent being given off by the surrounding flowers.

Clive guided Sarah down to the soft grass and momentarily broke away from her soft lips. "No one will be out here this afternoon," he said, gazing into Sarah's emerald green eyes. She knew there was no way that he could truly know that, but suddenly she didn't care. She didn't care who might see them; she didn't care about her agenda. Sarah's mind clouded over with an indescribable need to feel Clive's body against hers. She arched her neck to meet Clive's lips once again and pulled him the rest of the way down to her.

Out of the corner of his eye, Clive caught the reflection of the sun bouncing off a white marble statue that stood just a few feet from where Sarah and he were now lying. The statue was one of the most magnificent in the garden. It depicted a spirited mare who symbolized both spiritual power and physical strength. Along with the mare were her twin foals, one lying beneath her mother and the other standing next to her. The name etched upon the statue read "Alyssa Walker".

CHAPTER 12

March 27, 1042 AD - The chill of the wind slapped against Lord Artair's face as he and his men rode through the eastern lands of the Holy Roman Empire. It had been three years since he had last returned to his home in Northern Scotland, and too often did thoughts of regret and sorrow fill his troubled mind.

At first, it appeared as though a glorious miracle had occurred when Tyra survived the werewolf's bite and did not become infected herself. It was a miracle that Artair and Tyra eventually celebrated by marrying. After learning of Avonmora's death during her abduction by werewolves and Keara having disappeared under the dark shadow of the demon army, Artair and Tyra sought a new start by conceiving a child together. Their hope of a new beginning, however, died the night their son was born. Not only was Tyra's life lost during her labor, but it was discovered soon after that she had passed the unseen werewolf illness on to their newborn son, Doran.

HALLOWS END

A few months after Tyra's burial, Artair decided that he could not be a father to his "were-child" son and left his homeland to resume his search for Keara. In his stead, Artair left Diarmad in charge of both his castle and his lands, appointing the young soldier as the new Guardian of the North. Artair did ensure, however, that Doran would be cared for and raised under a watchful eye in hopes that the boy would eventually master control over his curse.

During Artair's last visit home, he had charged Diarmad with the task of organizing a small group of entrusted soldiers and spiritual leaders to protect humanity against the immortal races. Artair's heart had grown cold with distrust, and he feared that one day the demon armies would rise against the rest of the world. This covenant of men called themselves the "Order of the North".

Artair broke from his thoughts and addressed Sir Gordan. "We approach the outcast's stronghold," he said gruffly, pointing to the short mountain range where it was rumored that Dominious now lived in exile. The Demon lord had fallen out of favor with his King Renner and was vulnerable to attack. "Our spies tell us their number is less than fifty. Kill all of them, but leave Dominious for my wrath."

"As you command, my Lord," Gordan replied as he led their small army through the open field toward the mountain scape. The aging knight had remained by Artair's side through the darker days that had been brought upon them, swearing both life and sword that he would help his Lord find Keara. As their army neared the base of the mountain range they spotted a small barracks with a dozen or so demon soldiers keeping watch.

Before the demons were able to sound their warning call, Artair's archers planted arrows into the hearts of their lookouts. Demon soldiers were extremely strong, but often times clumsy and slow, especially in the daylight. With the demons' remaining guard in disarray, Artair and Gordan rushed the pack and quickly dispensed of the rest.

"They will have better defenses inside their cave," Artair advised as his men stood ready.

Gordan looked up at the sun beginning its journey toward the west. "The sun will only be our ally for another hour, my Lord. If we do not act now, they will strike under the night's cover when our sight is diminished and theirs is at full strength."

"Well, we can't burn them out…" Artair thought out loud as he searched his mind for a means of luring the demons out. Ever since his first encounter with Dominious, Artair had spent a great deal of time studying the tales of the ancient races so that he might better understand his enemy.

"I've got an idea," he said with a sly grin as he walked up to the entrance of the cave. "I, Lord Artair of Scotland," he called out boisterously, "do challenge the mightiest warrior of your horde to a Battle to the death!" He hoped that while Dominious no longer held honor, that the rest of his demon clan would still respect the tradition of "Amasha Rukar". As was practiced by their forefathers, a single warrior of their enemy could challenge the greatest warrior amongst the demons to a battle to the death. Whoever the victor, the opposing side would surrender.

"I accept!" shouted a deep, raspy voice from within the cave. A giant demon warrior came charging from the cave, standing over seven feet tall and twice the width of Artair. "Arrgh!" the demon grunted as he swung his axe in an attempt to remove the Scottish Lord's head. Artair ducked the demon's swing and distanced himself so that he could evaluate his opponent.

The monster wore neither armor nor shirt. His eyes blazed and his skin flared red like fire. In their normal state, a demon's skin tone was an ash gray color, but during battle their skin turned bright crimson. The demon warrior let out another yell as he again rushed toward Artair with a second attempt at his head.

"Woosh." This time the blade missed by only a couple of inches. While Artair knew this method of attack would eventually wear the demon warrior out, he wasn't sure he would survive that many attempts. The demon came in for a third attempt, only this time he aimed for the body with a swing that would surely have cut the Lord in half. Artair managed to get his sword in front of the demon's axe, but the might of the demon's swing sent him flying several feet on to his back.

"We shall dine on your soldiers' flesh tonight," the demon taunted as he prepared for his final attack. "And I shall suck the eye balls from your skull to celebrate!"

Artair jumped to his feet and readied his blade. The demon monster came in with an undercutting motion that was meant to split the Lord from groin to skull, but it was the wrong move. Artair swiftly side-stepped the demon's massive axe and slashed quickly with his own sword. The scream of agony that came from the demon echoed through the mountains as the demon's right arm fell to the ground with the axe still clutched in its fist.

With the demon having fallen to his knees from shock, Artair ended his enemy's cries with a powerful stroke of his sword, sending the demon's head flying. His rage ceased momentarily as he wiped the spattered demon blood from his face.

"Your champion is defeated!" he shouted into the black abyss of the cave's opening. "Honor your ancestors and hold true to the code of 'Amasha Rukar'."

Several minutes passed before two dozen demon soldiers came walking out of the cave and into the sun light. They were unarmed and remained silent as they lined up in single file in front of Artair's soldiers. One of the demons, most likely the highest ranking officer, grunted a command in their ancient language and all of them kneeled with their heads bowed. It was demon custom when giving themselves up to present their necks for a swift death.

Artair raised his eyes to the sky for a sign from his God. He struggled with his religion these days, but rather than go back to his ancestor's Pagan beliefs, he more frequently chose to believe in nothing at all. He spotted a vulture hovering not far from their site and decided that was enough of a sign for him. There was a day that the great Lord of the North would never have executed a man or any being who had given himself up honorably on the battlefield; however, today was not that day. He gave the signal to Gordan and as Artair walked toward the cave's entrance, he heard the steel of his soldiers' blades making contact with flesh and bone.

The cave was not deep, for Artair had to walk only a few paces before he could see the light of a fire. As he neared, he saw Dominious kneeling by the fire, the demon's face mostly obscured by his black cloak. "Why do you not give yourself up like your fellow brethren?" Artair asked, moving closer to the demon lord.

"I gave up a long time ago, Lord Artair," Dominious replied in a calm tone. "I simply chose the warmth of a fire over the cold field of battle to live my final moments." His cordial demeanor did nothing to calm the rage within Artair's heart. The Scottish Lord wanted answers and was eager to cause pain for their forthcoming. He lunged toward Dominious, placing both of his hands around the demon's neck and forcing Dominious' face closer to the flames.

"I know what you seek," Dominious choked out, not giving any resistance to his aggressor. "You need not torture me. I will tell you whatever you like."

Artair was frustrated with his own foolish attempt to make Dominious talk, since demons weren't actually affected by fire. His chest heaved furiously as he released the demon lord and took a moment to gather himself. "Why did you send the wolves after us?" he barked.

"The child you gave to me that day bore the mark of Lemuria, the ancient kingdom of my race," Dominious answered as he settled himself back in front of the soothing heat of the fire. "I knew you were hiding something from me, for the child of prophecy was supposed to bear the mark of Atlantis as well. That is why I sent the werewolf spies after your party. I wanted to know what secrets you were keeping."

"Your beast slaves killed her!" Artair shouted, pacing back and forth within the small confines of the cave.

"I imagine from your viewpoint that you refer not only to the child bearing the Atlantis mark, but to the Celtic witch who bore the children of prophecy as well?" Dominious questioned as he stared at the fire.

"Only a handful of my werewolf spies survived the attack on your camp that night. On their way back to my legion, the werewolves did not show enough care in eluding your King's army and they were captured. The child you referred to as Avonmora, still alive in the werewolves' keep, was put to death immediately at the order of your King Malcolm II."

"Liar!" Artair shouted as he drew his sword and raised it above the demon's head. He did not want to believe that his own king would betray him; though over time he had grown suspicious of the King of Scotland.

King Malcolm II had acted indifferent over the death of Avonmora, telling Artair they had discovered her broken body next to a stream after slaughtering the werewolf spies. Artair found it extremely odd that a king who found it so important to find the child of prophecy would show so little remorse over her death.

"I have no reason to lie to you, Lord Artair," Dominious retorted, not even flinching while the blade was centered directly above his skull. "You can kill me whenever you like, but I imagine you would also like to know what happened to the other child, Keara?"

Artair stayed the blade in his hands. "What of Keara?" he asked as he prepared his heart for yet another slough of sickening news.

"She lives," Dominious stated with a raised eyebrow. Artair took a step back, his sword falling to his side. In truth, he had only allowed himself to hope for the truth about Keara's death; he had never expected to learn that she survived.

"About 2,500 years ago," Dominious continued, "my ancestor, the great Lord Brakkus, made a deal with the Dark Queen Odessa to retrieve the child of prophecy for her. In exchange for the child, Odessa would give him the weapon our army needed to take Earth back from the race of humans. It was his dream to rebuild the great kingdom of Lemuria and bring about a new age for all our people."

Lord Artair's face grew impatient with Dominious' storytelling. "What about Keara?" he bellowed.

"When you handed the child over to me, I ignored my King Renner's orders and instead I took Keara to Odessa in order to fulfill Brakkus' end of the deal. Unfortunately, the Dark Queen knew of your lies before I did. She took Keara, but would not give me the weapon I sought until I had delivered Avonmora to her as well. Queen Odessa informed me that she required both halves of the now divided spirit of Lucifer's and Navaia's unborn child. Obviously that turned out to be an impossible task after your King Malcolm II had Avonmora killed."

Dominious removed the black cloak from his head to reveal a symbol branded upon the top of his skull. "When I returned to King Renner without the child or the weapon, he branded me a failure and I was cast out by my own people."

"Am I supposed to feel sorry for you, Demon?" Artair questioned as the anger began to swell in his eyes again.

"I suppose not." Dominious replaced the cloak over his hairless grey head. "You think that only you have suffered loss, yet because of you, I failed my entire race. I'd say we're even, Lord Artair."

Artair ignored the demon's last comment, his mind now focused on rescuing Keara. "Tell me where I can find the Dark Queen!" he commanded.

Dominious took a deep breath, fully aware that the next words he spoke would be his last. "Queen Odessa and her fellow Lamiai reside in the Black Peak of the great mountain range to the East. Be warned, however. The Dark Queen is a great sorceress who cannot be defeated by the likes of you. You, and the soldiers who foolishly follow you, will lose your mortal lives as well as your souls. You will die a failure...like me."

"There are much worse fates than death," Artair said, tightening his grip around his sword. Flames shimmered in the reflection of the steel as he lowered his blade down upon the suspecting demon lord. Dominious' head rolled into the fire as the rest of his lifeless body fell to the side.

"Sir Gordan!" Artair shouted, emerging from the cave. "Prepare the men. We ride for the Black Peak of the forbidden mountain range."

"My Lord." Gordan looked confused. "What do we hope to find there?"

"Redemption!" Lord Artair responded.

CHAPTER 13

Sarah reached out to ring the doorbell at Dr. Nemitz' enormous Victorian style house. The outside of his home was painted a dark shade of violet with black trim around the windows. There were mystical beasts carved into the wood railings on the steps and porch, much like the buildings downtown, and an etching of a large black eagle on the front door.

"Good evening, Ms. Chase." Dr. Nemitz greeted Sarah with an enthusiastic smile, ushering her into the entry way. The interior of the house featured dark, auburn wood floors with cherry wood furniture and violet curtains. The item, however, that caught Sarah's eye the most was the bannister on the long, winding staircase leading from the second story to the entry way. The handrail featured the carving of wild horses running from the top of the stairs to the bottom where she was now standing. Sarah had always been fond of horses though she hadn't ridden in years.

Dr. Nemitz hung Sarah's jacket on the coat rack and escorted her past the staircase into the dining room on the left. The room was lit brilliantly by a crystal chandelier hanging from the slightly elevated ceiling, and all of the curtains were pulled open so that the park across the street was in full view.

"Dinner won't be ready for a few more minutes," Dr. Nemitz said as he cheerfully uncorked the bottle of Pinot Noir he had referenced in the morning, "but the wine is ready to pour right now."

As the doctor offered Sarah a glass of wine, she noticed there were three place settings at the large dining room table. "Will the chef be joining us tonight?" she inquired.

"Oh, Rosemary? Not tonight...though we will have another guest joining us shortly. I only asked Rosemary to prepare dinner tonight because I'm a rather horrible cook and I didn't want to scare you away." He chuckled as he raised his wine glass toward Sarah and took a drink.

Sarah's eyebrows furrowed at the mention of 'another guest'. "Who else will be joining us?"

"It's a surprise," Dr. Nemitz responded with a wink. "Though I can tell you it's someone who has very much been looking forward to meeting you."

"Really?" Sarah exclaimed, doing her best to play it off like she was intrigued about Dr. Nemitz' mystery guest. In reality, the idea of a surprise dinner guest put her even more on edge. Sarah could tell he was hiding something, and even though he seemed like a decent guy on the outside, she knew all too well that often the darkest souls take refuge in those who appear to be the kindest.

"So, what did you do today in Hallows End?" the doctor inquired, looking quite content with his wine glass in hand.

"Well, after I dropped by the very interesting Candy Shoppe," Sarah's eyes widened to accentuate the word 'interesting', "I went to the gym and bumped into that guy Clive from the diner. He volunteered to show me around town so we spent the rest of the day visiting the shops and taking in the scenery." Sarah omitted her visit to the Sheriff's office, though she assumed Diana had probably already told him.

"I trust Clive was a good host then?" Dr. Nemitz asked in a fatherly tone.

"He was." Sarah smiled. She intended to be a pleasant guest, but her own agenda for the evening was to figure out exactly what the Doctor knew about the black Suburban and Stanley.

"Clive showed me the Garden of Spirits. Quite impressive the way your town recognizes those who have passed." Sarah's mind briefly re-visited her afternoon with Clive in the Garden, and she felt her skin become slightly warmer at the thought of him on top of her in the grass.

"You visited the Garden of Spirits?" Dr. Nemitz said with a look of surprise. "Well, if you liked that, you'll have to visit the library tomorrow. It's a magnificent building, built in the image of the great Imperial Library of Austria."

Sarah nodded and was about to re-visit the topic of the black Suburban when the doorbell rang.

"I'll be right back." He set his glass down on the table and walked to the front door.

Sarah felt an odd energy in the air and readied herself to meet the surprise guest. She lowered her arm slightly so that it was close to the gun she had hidden under her pants leg. She was fully prepared in case it was Stanley Jones who ended up walking into the dining room. It was somewhat of a leap to think that Dr. Nemitz would actually bring the werewolf over to confront her in the doctor's home, but "monster hunters" couldn't afford to take chances.

If Stanley was the 'surprise guest', Sarah had plenty of silver bullets to disable him so that she could then sever his head with the knife she was concealing under her other pant leg. Sarah considered a scenario where Dr. Nemitz might interfere with her taking Stanley down and, if the doctor tried, Sarah wouldn't hesitate in planting a bullet in his forehead as well.

With her ear fixed on what was happening in the entry way, Sarah heard Dr. Nemitz greeting his guest along with the sound of a female's voice responding back to him.

She considered the possibility that the woman could be Elise, especially since Diana had told her that Elise was Dr. Nemitz' daughter.

Sarah remained in a position to defend herself, but much to her relief it wasn't necessary. As Dr. Nemitz came back into the dining room he was accompanied by a blonde woman who looked young enough to be the doctor's granddaughter. She was wearing a royal blue blouse with black pants and a long pony tail that reached past her lower back. Sarah pretended to scratch her calf as she casually brought her right hand back up to her lap.

"Sarah, I want you to meet our guest tonight. This is Sadeana." Dr. Nemitz left the woman's side and made his way back to the chair at the head of the table. He watched intently while the two exchanged pleasantries.

"Nice to meet you." Sarah looked at the fair-skinned, blue-eyed woman in front of her, and couldn't help but feel like there was something incredibly familiar about her. She stood up to shake hands with Sadeana and as their palms touched, a tremendous shiver pulsated through her body. Sarah released the young woman's hand abruptly and took a step back.

"It's a pleasure," Sadeana replied, seemingly unfazed by Sarah's sudden withdrawal. She walked over to the other side of the dining room table and sat down next to Dr. Nemitz. "My full name," she continued as she looked directly into Sarah's eyes, "is Sadeana Walker."

HALLOWS END

As soon as the last name 'Walker' departed from Sadeana's lips, Sarah froze. She now understood why Sadeana seemed so familiar. Even though she didn't have any of their mother's dark features, there was no denying how similar their faces looked. The young woman was, without a doubt, the daughter of Alyssa Walker. Sarah slowly lowered herself back into her chair, raw with uncertainty as to how she would handle this new turn of events.

"Alyssa Walker was your mother?" Sarah already knew the answer, but she wanted to hear Sadeana say it all the same.

"She was," Sadeana responded softly. "and I'm sorry that she was never able to return to Portland and tell you about me."

Sarah paused for a moment, thinking to herself that she wished her mother had told her about Sadeana as well. "So...you're too young to be the reason my mother left Portland...but I'm guessing you were the reason she didn't come back?" Sarah's tone didn't reflect anger or accusation. She was simply stunned and curious.

"In a way." Sadeana seemed to struggle to find the words that would help Sarah understand. "What I'm about to tell you might seem rather unbelievable, but I assure you it's the truth." Sarah made no attempt to interrupt as she was eager for an explanation.

"I was born on the 26th day of December, 1975 to Alyssa Walker. According to legend, I am the reincarnation of Avonmora, one of the twin sisters of prophecy born in the year 1033 AD in Scotland." Sadeana stood up, unbuttoned part of her blouse, and lowered it so that her shoulders and upper back were exposed. She then turned around to reveal a bright blue circle with a trident inside of it on the middle of her upper back. The symbol glowed as if there were an electrical current running through it.

"It is the symbol of the ancient kingdom of Atlantis," Sadeana explained as she buttoned her blouse up and sat back down in her chair. "Our mother brought me here so Dr. Nemitz could keep me hidden from those who would use my power for evil."

"Okay…" Sarah said, not necessarily believing the story that Sadeana was telling her, but also having no idea why she would be making it up. "You're telling me then, that even though you barely look twenty, that you're actually my older sister?" Sarah spoke with a rather thick tone of cynicism in her voice.

"I'm told the reason I don't age the same as humans is because, technically, I'm only half human." Sadeana broke eye contact with Sarah and looked down at the table, embarrassed. She had practiced her speech thousands of times, but now felt she was coming up short in convincing her sister of the truth.

"You see," Dr. Nemitz interjected, "the children of prophecy are conceived only between spirit and their mother, so Sadeana has no human father."

Of course she doesn't, Sarah thought to herself. Although she spent her free time hunting werewolves and vampires, Sarah wasn't one to buy into far-fetched tales. She reached for her glass of wine, decided to skip delving any further into Sadeana's back story and proceeded with her next question.

"Why didn't our mother stay in Hallows End with you?" Sarah directed her inquiry at her sister, but it was Dr. Nemitz who answered.

"Your mother fell in love with the man whom I had sent to protect them when Sadeana was first born. They lived in Hallows End together, for a while, but he was drawn off to another mission and no one ever heard from him again. A few days after he left, your mother discovered that she was pregnant…with you."

Sarah's heart raced at her father being mentioned. Her mother had never spoken about him nor had she ever been given any explanation for his absence from her life. Sarah was tempted to change course and ask about what happened to her father, but decided to reserve that question for later.

"That doesn't explain why our mother left Hallows End though. Why didn't she just raise us together, here?" This time Sarah was looking right at Dr. Nemitz when she posed her question.

"Your mother didn't want to raise her children in Hallows End. However, she also knew that Sadeana was not safe outside of the protection I could provide for your sister here. So, your mother made the difficult choice of leaving Sadeana in Hallows End under my care and moving to Portland to start a new life with you."

"But she didn't stay in Portland, did she?" Sarah said pointedly. "She left my step-father and me and never came back…why?"

"There were threats," he said, finishing his glass and then pouring another. "Different 'interest groups' were looking for your sister. I sent a message to your mother that I planned to move Sadeana to a more secure location. Unfortunately, your mother responded by coming here."

Dr. Nemitz allowed his eyes to drift down to the table momentarily. "Through no fault of hers, things became worse after she arrived and her returning to Portland would have put both you and your step-father in great danger. Your mother loved you, Sarah," Dr. Nemitz stated gently. "She wanted to return to you…it just wasn't safe."

"If it was so dangerous for my mother to return to Portland, then what am I doing here?" The tone of Sarah's voice had become harsh. She realized now it was no coincidence that she had ended up in Hallows End, and any feelings of sadness or loss that she had been harboring were turning to anger. "What makes today so special that I finally get to know the truth about my mother's disappearance and my secret, half-human sister?"

"I swore an oath to your mother a long time ago," Dr. Nemitz looked back into Sarah's piercing gaze, "that I would help protect both of her daughters."

"Like you protected her?" Sarah said abruptly.

Dr. Nemitz paused for a second, the sting of Sarah's words striking his core. He knew in his heart that he was partially to blame for Alyssa Walker's death. "Ever since your mother passed away, I've been keeping a close watch on you. From your graduating high school to your rapid ascension as a police detective, and everything in between...and I know the reason you've come to Hallows End is because you're tracking a werewolf who goes by the name of Stanley Jones."

"Then you know the reason I followed Stanley to Hallows End is to kill him." Sarah still had a lot of questions she wanted answered, but in her mind, finding Stanley had to take precedent over her personal life; at least for now.

"Trust me, Stanley will have to answer for his actions," Dr. Nemitz assured Sarah, "but there are much more important things occurring right now."

"Trust you?" Sarah's temper finally boiled over. "I have a pretty good feeling you're the last person I should trust in this town! After all, I'm guessing you planted that murdering son-of-a-bitch in Portland knowing that I would track him down and that he would eventually lead me to Hallows End!"

"Please, Sarah," Dr. Nemitz tried to explain, "I admit, I allowed Stanley to move to Portland and try civilian life again because you lived in the same city. However, my intent was to tip you off to his presence, alert Stanley that he had been 'identified', and then have you follow him back to Hallows End. I had no reason to believe that he would begin killing innocent women."

"He's a fucking werewolf!" Sarah shouted as she leaned over the table toward Dr. Nemitz. "I don't know exactly what you hoped to accomplish tonight, but right now I'm getting the hell out of here and I'm taking Stanley Jones down!" Sarah got up from the table, grabbed her leather jacket and slammed the front door behind her.

CHAPTER 14

From the Journal of Sadeana Walker, August 19, 2013

At last the day has come for me to meet my sister, Sarah. Though I have often times thought about what it would be like to meet her, last night was the first time that I can remember having such a vivid dream about the journey that she and I will be embarking upon. I wonder, when the moment comes for me to face the evil I was born to vanquish, if Sarah will be able to stand by without risking her own life to save me. I'm not sure that I would be up to the challenge if the roles were reversed.

For so many years now I have lived in Hallows End, training for an enemy I have never seen, swearing to protect the lives of both humans and immortals, though I have few friends to count among them. Dr. Nemitz has taught me so much in the way of wisdom and knowledge, yet it is love, I'm told, that gives life its greatest meaning. For me, whose life has been void of love since the passing of my mother, I fear that I have lost touch with the most important reason for carrying out my impending quest.

Perhaps it will be Sarah who can help me to remember what love is. I imagine that it will be a natural feeling to love my sister. I know that she may harbor feelings of resentment toward me for our mother having left her when she was so young. No matter how many words I offer her as explanation, I will never be able to fully portray the pain and guilt that mother felt every day for having left Sarah in Portland. However, I do hope that she will be able to forgive me for such things that were beyond either of our control.

I must admit, I feel rather unprepared for dinner tonight even though Dr. Nemitz and I have gone over my lines a thousand times. I can only imagine what Sarah will think when I tell her that I have no father and that I was born to our mother by way of a spiritual power I myself still don't understand. After all, I look human. My mother was human. I'm told that the child whose spirit flows through my veins was Atlantian, yet I have none of the special powers that Atlantians possessed.

Josh, one of my trainers, says that I do have a special power, but it doesn't seem like anything particularly remarkable. He references the fact that I can anticipate the future, but it's only by a couple of seconds; nothing all that useful except in combat. I must admit though, I do like the advantage it seems to give me over others when fighting. In fact, I've even been besting Josh in our duels lately.

HALLOWS END

Dr. Nemitz just came by to see how I was doing. He worries about me; he knows that he will not be able to guide or protect me in the next phase of my life. He seems to believe that Sarah will protect me, which I find somewhat unusual since I am the older and more powerful sister. It's not that I don't appreciate the notion of having someone look out for me, but I would imagine that Josh or Mason would make better bodyguards.

Well, the time is drawing close for me to get ready for tonight's dinner. I think it's a little silly that I am to ring the doorbell to my own home, but Dr. Nemitz insisted that I come through the front door. He also chose this ridiculous looking shirt for me to wear; it looks like something of Rosemary's! Oh well, I suppose it's really not that important how I'm dressed.

I believe I will confer with my fortune cards before I set out. They have never steered me wrong and are a welcome complement to my ability to see the future. I'm not necessarily worried about how the evening will go, but perhaps the cards will help guide me down a better path than I would have chosen on my own.

CHAPTER 15

The partially lit moon was close to full height in the night's sky by the time the lights in Lucifer's Garden began turning on. Sarah stood up from the park bench she had been sitting on for the past three hours and headed toward the club's entrance across the street. Being alone had given her some time to 'digest' the events that had transpired at Dr. Nemitz' house, and she was regretting now that she had left before asking more questions.

There was a part of Sarah that believed the stories Dr. Nemitz and Sadeana were telling her. After all, she had spent her entire life wondering what had happened to her mother, who her father was, and what other myths in addition to vampires and werewolves were true. As Sarah stood waiting for someone to open the front door of the club, she resolved to go back to Dr. Nemitz' house the next day and attempt another conversation.

HALLOWS END

A muscular man with a shaved head opened the door to the night club and smiled as he looked Sarah up and down in a suggestive manner. Sarah immediately recognized him as the 'man in black' from the night of Stanley's abduction.

"May I help you?" the man asked with a flirtatious grin. His teeth were as perfect as his meticulously trimmed goatee and his black t-shirt was quite purposefully two sizes too small for him.

"She's with me, Brutus," a voice said from behind.

Sarah turned around and saw Clive walking toward her. She suspected Clive's 'hospitality' earlier in the day had been somehow orchestrated by Dr. Nemitz, and she wasn't in the mood for distractions. Clive reached out for her, but Sarah shrugged him off and turned her attention back to Brutus.

"No, I'm not," Sarah clarified. "My name is Detective Sarah Chase and I'm here on official police business. I need to speak with the manager of your club." Sarah briefly turned toward Clive again to flash him a 'get the hell away from me' glare.

"You wanna meet Elise, huh?" Brutus asked, his voice about an octave deeper than most men Sarah had met. He raised his right arm to pretend like he was scratching his head to stop and think about her request, but it was quite obvious he just wanted to flex his massive bicep for Sarah's admiration.

"She's not at the club yet," Brutus said casually, still flexing his bicep, "but I can take you to a table to wait for her."

"Thank you," Sarah replied. Knowing that she had found one half of the duo from the night of Stanley's abduction gave Sarah confidence that she was on the right track to catch Stanley. As she followed Brutus into the club, Clive reached out for her in protest, but this time he was met with a stiff shove from Brutus.

"Doesn't appear the lady's in the mood for your company tonight, Clive," Brutus said with his chest puffed out. Brutus stood six inches taller than Clive and his hulking frame was in stark contrast to Clive's slender build. Clive backed off, but rather than leave, he went across the street and sat on the bench where Sarah had been.

Sarah considered that it might have been a safer move to allow Clive to follow her into the club considering the entire place could be crawling with 'blood suckers' and werewolves. However, it was hard to believe that Dr. Nemitz would go to so much trouble to bring Sarah to Hallows End and then let her be killed.

The inside of the club was decorated in a combination of red paint and black upholstery with large tropical foliage and jungle props strewn about. The bar stood in the middle with booths set up on the side walls and a large dance floor at the front. Techno metal pulsated from the speakers as Sarah followed Brutus past the hanging cages on the dance floor to a table near the bar.

Brutus motioned to one of the waitresses to come over to Sarah's table. "I'll tell Elise you're here when she arrives."

Brutus' demeanor had suddenly become more professional and authoritative now that he was in view of the other club employees. "I've got to get back to my post, but Marin will get you something while you wait." Brutus left Sarah's table just as the waitress, Marin, came over.

"He's pretty sexy, huh?" Marin said with a lustful grin as she watched Brutus' backside exiting the club. Marin looked like she had just stepped out of the cabaret. She had red ribbons in her long curly hair, matching red lipstick and a very short black and red skirt. "Haven't seen you in here before, Sweetie. You new in town?"

"Just passing through," Sarah replied.

Out of the corner of her eye Sarah watched for anyone who looked like the woman she had seen from the Suburban.

"Who ya' lookin' for?" Marin asked with a grin. "I know a few guys who'd be interested if you're looking for some fun tonight."

"I'm actually waiting to talk to your manager, Elise," Sarah said, moving her gaze from the entrance to Marin. "Would you please let me know as soon as she arrives?"

"Sure thing, sugar." Marin began twirling her long brown curls with her right hand. "Can I get you something while you wait?"

"No, thank you," Sarah replied as she again turned her attention to scanning the room.

Sarah's suspicions as to what kind of customer Lucifer's Garden was attracting were confirmed as people started entering the club. Most of them looked like they were in their 20's and 30's, and were dressed more for a drug-enhanced rave than a small town night club. Sarah clearly understood now why the club was called 'Lucifer's Garden'.

As Marin departed, Sarah was aware that another woman was walking toward her. A curvy brunette wearing a sheer, skin-tight black dress approached. Sarah recognized her as the woman who had helped Brutus abduct Stanley.

"Ms. Chase," the woman stated flatly. Her lipstick was dark as red wine and the material of her dress was so transparent that it was obvious she had decided against wearing underwear for the night. "My name is Elise Cunning."

"Hello, Ms. Cunning," Sara replied as she stood up from the booth. "I'm here…"

"My bouncer," Elise interrupted, "told me there was a police officer in my club who wanted to ask me a few questions." She stood in front of Sarah with her arms crossed and an extremely agitated expression on her face.

"Martin recommended I come by and see you tonight. I was tracking a man down the 101 last night near the Hallows End exit when my car went off the road. He was driving a black Suburban..."

"So your car just went off the road?" Elise interrupted Sarah again, her tone of voice harboring a thick amount of condescension. "All by itself?"

Sarah felt the urge to knock Elise out, but took a deep breath and started again. "Ms. Cunning, I'm a police detective from Portland and I'm tracking a man who's suspected of murder. I would appreciate you giving me any information that could help me find the man."

"Are you sure it's a man you're looking for?" Elise asked with a sly grin.

"Yes," Sarah responded, refusing to take the bait. She assumed that both Elise and Brutus knew what Stanley really was. After all, Dr. Nemitz had all but admitted to orchestrating Stanley's abduction so that Sarah would follow them to Hallows End. However, she didn't want to let on too much and give Elise the upper hand in their conversation.

"Well, I haven't seen a black Suburban, so I guess I can't help you."

Sarah was getting frustrated with Elise's games. "Have you or any of your employees…"

"No, we haven't," Elise cut Sarah off once again. "Now, as stimulating as this conversation has been, I need to get back to managing my club." Elise turned her back to Sarah and walked to the entrance, greeting guests on her way.

Sarah was about to follow after Elise when Marin returned with a drink on her tray. "Jack and Cherry Coke on the rocks," she said, placing a napkin and the drink on Sarah's table.

Sarah looked down at the drink with the maraschino cherry nestled on top of the ice. "Uh, I didn't order this," she said, confused as to why Marin brought it to her, but also wondering how it was the waitress knew what her drink of preference was.

"I know," Marin replied, this time with an innocent sweetness shining through her suggestive appearance. "But it's your favorite and I figured you could use it."

Sarah looked down at the drink once more and decided to find out if her mind-reading waitress knew anything. "Unusual for a small town to have so many night owls, isn't it?" she asked, taking a sip of her drink.

"The town feels pretty small during the day," Marin explained. "However, come night time, a lot of the townsfolk who live in the apartments above the storefronts come out."

"And yet it seemed so quiet during the day while I was walking around town. Where were all of these people then?" Sarah saw the look of contemplation on Marin's face and knew she was breaking through the illusion of Hallows End.

"Dr. Nemitz founded this town as a sort of haven for people," Marin replied, her words having become so soft that Sarah was pretty much having to read her lips to understand her. "No one gets judged for their lifestyles, but Dr. Nemitz does ask that they keep their controversial sides private during the day."

"Controversial?" Sarah asked, hoping Marin would give something away.

"I probably shouldn't be telling you this, considering you're a cop," Marin leaned in to Sarah slightly "but there's quite a few residents here who have sordid pasts." As soon as the words had left her mouth Marin became very conscious that she had been talking to Sarah for quite a while and that others in the club had most likely taken notice.

Sarah could tell that Marin was about to bolt. "Have you seen or heard anything about a black Suburban driving into town in the last 24 hours or so?"

"Oooh, I'm afraid I can't comment," Marin replied. "In fact, I shouldn't even be standing here. Sorry." She quickly turned away and left.

Sarah watched Marin head back to the bar and noticed Elise standing next to the far corner booth near the exit. There were three people sitting at the booth, and Sarah almost jumped out of her skin when she saw who one of them was.

"Holy shit!" Sarah exclaimed, though the words came out as only a murmur under her breath. Elise was standing right next to Stanley Jones. Sarah knew her approaching him could cause a scene, but she didn't care.

Elise had been watching Marin and Sarah's conversation and was now relishing the effect Stanley's presence was having on the Detective. Sarah had her badge out and was almost to Stanley's booth when Elise stepped in front of her.

"What do you think you're doing, Ms. Chase?" Elise snarled.

"Enough bullshit!" Sarah shouted as she leaned to Elise's right just enough that she could make eye contact with Stanley. "Stanley Jones. You are under arrest for the murder of Emily Fisher."

Panic flitted over Stanley's face, but he remained still. Sarah made a move for her gun, but before she could pull it out, two enormous hands grabbed her arms, immobilizing her.

"Is there a problem here, Elise?" Brutus asked as he held Sarah with strength she had never encountered before. Sarah could have sworn that Brutus was still outside; otherwise she would have been prepared for him.

"I'm afraid Ms. Chase is being quite rude, Brutus," Elise said as she stared right into Sarah's eyes.

"Let go of me, you son of a bitch!" Sarah tried to free herself with no luck. "I'm a fucking cop!"

"Who's out of her jurisdiction," Elise added snidely. "Brutus, please escort Ms. Chase out of our club. She is no longer welcome."

Just as Brutus began to drag Sarah toward the door, Elise grabbed Sarah's arm and looked directly in her eyes. "Don't come back." Elise's eyes flickered red and fangs protruded past her gum line, revealing that she was a vampire.

Sara didn't flinch at Elise's display, but she did stop resisting Brutus' hold. Regardless of Dr. Nemitz' influence over the town, Sarah knew she couldn't take on an entire club full of vampires and werewolves. A peaceful exit to fight another day was all that Sarah could hope for at this point.

Brutus practically carried Sarah out of the club and released her once they were outside. "You're not a very smart lady," Brutus stated, shaking his head.

Clive had seen them exit the club and made his way hurriedly to Sarah's side. "Are you all right, Sarah?" he asked.

"I'm fine, Clive," Sarah said, gesturing for him to take a step back from her. "Just got in a little over my head." She downplayed the events since she didn't need Clive getting protective and making the situation worse. Suddenly, a very loud howl came from only a few feet away. Sarah knew exactly from what creature the howl had come from.

Clive looked at Sarah in alarm. "Run!" he yelled. Sarah paused for a second, considering the direction she should take, and decided the Sheriff's Station was her best chance. There was no way that Diana didn't know about the residents of Hallows End, and Sarah hoped the sheriff had an arsenal in the station for 'special occasions'. Sarah took off at a sprint and never looked back to see if Clive was following her. It wasn't that she didn't care; she just couldn't afford to spare the milliseconds it might cost her.

Clive watched Sarah run down the street toward the police station. He almost screamed out to her to go to Dr. Nemitz' mansion instead, but he knew she didn't have any chance of making it there before the werewolves caught her. As Clive turned to confront Brutus, he could hear wolves snarling behind him.

"She didn't mean anyone any harm," Clive said, attempting to control the situation. He looked down at Brutus' heels where four wolves had now congregated. "She was just doing her job."

"You know we abide by our own laws here," Brutus said with a cold stone face. The wolves took off in Sarah's direction as he knocked Clive out with a single punch to the side of the skull. Brutus could have easily killed Clive if he'd wanted to, but there were strict laws against killing a fellow resident in Hallows End and he wasn't ready to cross that line.

Sarah was three-quarters of the way to the station when she heard the wolves closing in behind her. She'd never make it to the station in time and even though she was no match for an entire pack of werewolves, she stopped in her tracks and turned to face her enemies.

The wolves were 50 feet behind her and slowed their pace as they closed in. Sarah continued to step backwards slowly as the wolves growled and inched toward her, all four moving in a synchronized attack formation.

"Come on, you bastards!" She shouted, hoping that someone might hear her. Sarah grabbed her firearm and pointed it at the wolf at the head of the pack. She might not be able to take out all four of them, but she refused to die without a fight.

As soon as the lead wolf broke from the pack and leapt toward her, Sarah fell back into a bicycle kick that sent him flying several feet behind her. She then unloaded her rounds quickly into the other three.

Sarah fired her final bullet and was about to reload when the lead wolf jumped her from behind and closed its jaws around her shoulder. Sarah was pinned down on the ground in agony while the other three wolves slowly regenerated from their wounds. Just as she was about to take her last breath, a gunshot rang through the night's air and the lead wolf's jaws went limp on Sarah's punctured shoulder.

She quickly freed herself from the jaws of the wolf and distanced herself as it transitioned back into its human form. She looked up to see Diana take a long sword and behead the man on the spot. The other three werewolves fled before the sheriff could exact the same punishment upon them.

"Thank you," Sarah said, with blood and white pus running down her shoulder. She wanted to say more, alert Diana to Clive's possible peril, tell her about Elise and Brutus, but she had no strength left. Sarah could feel the mutating poison from the werewolf's bite seeping through her wound and infecting her blood stream. She crawled a few inches toward Diana and passed out.

CHAPTER 16

"What the hell were you thinking, Elise?" Dr. Nemitz questioned angrily as Elise stood behind the steel bars in the dungeon beneath the Sheriff's office. Diana had immediately taken both her and Brutus into custody after getting Sarah back to Dr. Nemitz' house.

"I was thinking why the hell is there a human woman running around Hallows End unsupervised and making threats to our residents!" Elise snapped back angrily.

"Clive or I have been in Ms. Chase's company the entire time she's been in Hallows End," he retorted. "And, as for Stanley, I'm not sure we have any right protecting him from the law. He murdered two innocent girls."

"There is no such thing as an innocent human!" Elise was now shouting at the top of her lungs. "And I do believe Clive lost his babysitting privileges when he started fucking the..."

"Clive is not on trial here, Elise!" Dr. Nemitz said sternly, interrupting Elise's rant.

"Is that what this is? Am I seriously on trial for doing my job and protecting our town?"

"Of course you are. Your job is to ensure that the whereabouts of Hallows End and its residents remain safe and secret. It is not your place to wage an attack and attempt to murder a human who I specifically ordered was to remain unharmed."

Elise remained silent for a moment and looked at Diana standing behind Dr. Nemitz. "What the hell are you looking at?"

"A loose cannon," Diana responded in a monotone voice. Diana had never trusted Elise to take over the duties of the small task force that William Luse had been in charge of. She didn't push the issue with Dr. Nemitz however, because of his close relationship with Elise.

Dr. Nemitz spoke again to get Elise's attention off Diana. "You realize you got Travis killed, don't you? In the eyes of our laws that's the same as if you had killed Travis yourself."

"Bullshit!" Elise snarled back, still glaring at Diana. "She killed Travis!"

"Diana had no choice," he said, waving his finger in front of Elise's vision. "Travis would have killed Ms. Chase if Diana hadn't stopped him."

"Since when do we choose an outsider's life over the life of one of our own?" Elise moved her cold stare in the direction of Dr. Nemitz. "Oh, wait," she continued snidely, "I guess this actually wouldn't be the first time, now would it?"

"If you're referring to what happened years ago…"

"I know about the girl," Elise interrupted, not wanting to hear Dr. Nemitz' reference to the past. "I know she's the reason we've had a human in Hallows End before and I'm guessing that's why Ms. 'Bitch Cop' is here now."

Dr. Nemitz paused for a moment, slightly surprised that Elise knew about Sadeana. In all of the years she had been in Hallows End, Dr. Nemitz was quite sure that his cloaking spell on Sadeana had kept her from being visible to the other residents.

"The parlor tricks and deceptions of an old sorcerer aren't that difficult to overcome if you grow accustomed to them," Elise continued, the volume of her voice shifting down a few levels. "Is this girl really worth it? Last time we lost William; now we've lost Travis…"

"Travis is dead as a result of you directly disobeying my orders, Elise," Dr. Nemitz interjected, this time his voice breaking with anger. "You leave me no choice in the matter." He took a step back and tried to subdue his emotions so that he could deliver his judgment.

"The law of Hallows End is quite clear in this instance. Elise Cunning; you are hereby banished."

Elise said nothing. Dr. Nemitz broke his eye contact with her momentarily to briefly address Brutus who was standing behind her. "You may consider yourself banished as well, Brutus. You did nothing to stop the attack and you assaulted Clive so that he could not aide Ms. Chase."

"Diana will escort both of you from Hallows End tonight." Dr. Nemitz turned to leave the dungeon, but could not depart with his judgment being the last words he spoke to Elise.

He leaned in toward the bars with a whisper. "It breaks my heart to banish you, Elise. You were once like a daughter to me. I will never understand what I did to change things between us. What I did that made you so angry." Elise remained silent. Dr. Nemitz sighed and then walked out of the dungeon with Diana.

Upstairs and out of earshot, Diana and Dr. Nemitz sat down at the sheriff's desk and discussed their next move. "You realize that Elise is extremely dangerous, don't you?" Diana said to Dr. Nemitz.

"Yes."

"Albert, they can't be allowed to tell anyone about Hallows End or Sadeana. It would mean an end to everyone who lives here. It would undo everything you've tried to build." Diana reached across the desk and placed her hand upon Dr. Nemitz'. While her words hung heavy in the air, Diana's demeanor softened as they touched.

It wasn't a secret to anyone living in Hallows End that Dr. Nemitz and Diana loved one another. Although they had never married, the doctor and sheriff could often be seen dining together and holding hands while walking in the park.

"I'm not sure there's anything at this point that can prevent the outside world from discovering the whereabouts of Hallows End." Dr. Nemitz affectionately placed his other hand on Diana's. "Odessa is determined to find the child of prophecy and, as a result, we gain more enemies every day. Her demon spies have infiltrated every immortal community that we once counted as our allies. In fact, it wouldn't surprise me if Elise has already been in contact with a member of the demon legion."

"If that's true, then we cannot allow her and Brutus to leave Hallows End and show our enemies where it lies. Your magic may keep us hidden from outside eyes, but the illusion won't hold if the way in is shown to them."

"We must allow Elise and Brutus to leave Hallows End. It is our law and we have always held true to it." Dr. Nemitz released her hand and stood up slowly from the desk with what appeared to be a tremendous weight on his shoulders.

"However, you are also correct in that we must not allow them to reveal Hallows End to our enemies."

Dr. Nemitz stared deeply into Diana's eyes to ensure she caught on to his meaning.

"I understand," Diana replied. "I'll escort them out of Hallows End tonight. And come the dawn…the threat will be contained."

CHAPTER 17

"Do you think they suspect anything?" Brutus asked after Dr. Nemitz and Diana had left. The floor between the dungeon and the sheriff's office above had been built to ensure that no creature, not even a vampire, could hear through it.

"Yes," Elise responded nonchalantly. "In fact, I'm sure they're upstairs right now trying to decide whether or not to execute us."

"You believe the 'good Doctor' could really condemn you to death?"

"Maybe," Elise said with a devilish grin. "There was a time when I could have gotten away with anything, but I think the old man is finally ready to give up on me." Elise slowly paced back and forth in the cell, emphasizing the movement of her female form to ensure that Brutus took notice.

"It won't matter though," she continued. "Simeon and his army will be waiting for us right where I told him. We'll show them the way into Hallows End. They can take whatever item it is they seek, and then the town will be ours."

"You really feel comfortable allowing a bunch of demons to walk into Hallows End and look for something without knowing what it is they're searching for?"

Elise stopped pacing, frustrated that Brutus was analyzing her plan instead of paying attention to her seductive walk. "No, I don't feel comfortable with it, you idiot! Do you have a better idea on how to make this town ours?"

"No. I just don't see what the big rush is. Dr. Nemitz' health is fading and..."

"And even if he dies," Elise interrupted, "which I doubt he does anytime soon, that still leaves us with a Goddess in our way whom we can't defeat on our own! As much as I don't like the idea of demons running around our town, we can't take Hallows End without them."

"Do you think the demon army can really take out Diana? She's the last of her kind; she won't go down without a fight."

Elise rolled her eyes, her patience with Brutus having completely disappeared. "What the fuck, Brutus? Since when did you care so much about the god-damned plan? 'Yes', I think fifty demons can take care of one archaic bitch. And if it starts looking like they can't handle it, then we'll finish the job while she's distracted. Plenty of her kind have been killed by 'lesser' immortals; why do you think she's the last one?"

Brutus shrugged his shoulders slightly and moved in close to Elise. "Sorry; I shouldn't question your strategy. I know you've been planning this for a long time."

"I think you just like it when I'm pissed off," Elise teased as she placed her hands on his chest suggestively.

Brutus leaned in toward Elise, his fangs protruding from his mouth as he kissed her neck. "I just don't want us to wind up dead," he whispered.

"What's the difference if we have to continue pretending that our kind doesn't exist in the world?" Elise retorted as she used one of her fingernails to slowly tear the back of Brutus's shirt from the neckline to his waist. She then removed Brutus's shirt to reveal a massive, muscle-bound chest and eight-pack abs.

Brutus grinned at her seductive manner. "Do you really care about me, Elise?"

"Would you shut up already!" Elise commanded. She reached out, unbuttoned Brutus's pants, and flashed her fangs.

Brutus responded by pulling Elise's dress up to her waist and tearing the straps off her shoulders, allowing her breasts to spill over the top. He then hoisted her on top of him effortlessly. Their lips locked feverishly as their bodies writhed together with unbridled, inhuman passion.

CHAPTER 18

It was 2 AM by the time Diana walked down to the dungeon to retrieve Elise and Brutus. The smell of their vampire liaison in the air filled her nostrils and turned her stomach. Diana was not a fan of the vampire race, but because Dr. Nemitz had always been so close to Elise, she had done her best to learn to live with them.

"It's time," Diana said in a cold voice.

"Come, Brutus; let's get banished!" Elise laughed as she led a shirtless Brutus through the cell door by his belt buckle. She was relishing the thought of the trap that lay ahead for Diana.

The almost-full moon shone down upon the three of them as they walked through the downtown area and began their journey toward the border of Hallows End. Diana followed the two vampires closely, expecting that at some point in the evening Elise would try something.

"Lovely evening for a walk, isn't it?" Elise said to Brutus, her tone of voice dripping with malice. "Although," she continued, "there's some kind of foul scent upon the air…I believe it smells a bit like… betrayal." Elise's spirit filled with twisted delight at the double meaning of her words.

After some time, they crossed the border of Hallows End and continued on, deep into the redwood forest.

"Still following us, Diana?" Elise said as she turned her head slightly to look back in the Sheriff's direction. "Don't you trust us to leave peacefully?"

"I haven't trusted you in quite some time, Elise," Diana responded.

"I'm such a disappointment to my mother," Elise cackled sarcastically to Brutus.

"No daughter of mine would have ever tormented her father," Diana added with a rather angry tone.

Elise stopped walking, turned around and looked into Diana's eyes. "He was never my father!" Elise looked around the slight clearing they had come to. "Awfully far away from the border, aren't we?" she asked casually. "Makes a girl wonder if you ever plan on leaving us?"

"My job as the Sheriff of Hallows End is to escort you away from town," Diana responded matter-of-factly.

"What's your job as Dr. Nemitz' bitch though?" Elise posed with a horribly evil tone. Diana was a hard individual to faze, but Elise was starting to get under her skin.

"It didn't have to be this way, you know," Diana said, recognizing that the time had come to finish her assignment. She slowly removed the gun from her holster.

"Oh, my god!" Elise laughed. "Could you be any more cliché?"

"A couple of vampires are no match for me, Elise. I know you won't go peacefully, but I could spare you both the pain if you wished."

"Um, yeah, think I'll pass," Elise said mockingly. Suddenly, from out behind the trees marched a legion of demons."

Diana wasn't so much surprised by the presence of the demon soldiers as she was disappointed that it had come to this. "So…you sold out the people who loved and cared for you. For what, Elise?"

"I'm sure you'd like to know," Elise responded. "However, this isn't a movie and you don't get to know the plot before you die." With that Elise turned to Simeon, the leader of the demon army, and shouted a command at him. "Kill the Goddess!"

Diana looked up to the night's sky and closed her eyes. Her sheriff's uniform exploded off her body, sending shreds of clothing everywhere to reveal a skin-tight, golden armor beneath. A gold spear appeared in Diana's right hand as she charged the demon soldiers who were temporarily blinded by the magnificent light radiating from her body.

Thunder shook the ground as Diana tore through the demon army in a violent wave of severed limbs and showers of dark crimson blood. Her spear cut the demon's flesh with ease, but there were too many of them attacking her at once. As the demon soldiers continued to close in around her, Diana struggled to deflect the sting of their swords. Eventually, the biting of their steel tore through her Goddess skin.

Diana was the last of her kind on the planet; a direct descendant of the great Zeus and the "original" race of beings who first inhabited Earth. And while she was the mightiest warrior who had lived for the last thousand years, she knew this would be her final battle.

CHAPTER 19

As Sarah slowly came to consciousness she rolled her head to the side of her pillow and made out the shape of what appeared to be a man sitting in a chair across the room.

"Sarah?" the man said softly as he got up from his chair and reached out for her hand. Although she was still making sense of her surroundings, she recognized the man's gentle touch and knew it was Clive who was holding her hand.

She moved her head back to its original position and looked up at the dark ceiling above her. A few cracks of sunlight that had managed to peek through the curtains reflected off the walls, lighting the microscopic dust particles throughout the room. "Where am I?" she asked.

"We're in Dr. Nemitz' house," Clive answered, still holding Sarah's hand. "He wanted you moved here so that he could be absolutely sure you were safe."

Sarah questioned Clive's use of the word 'safe' considering the circumstances. She then remembered the werewolf attack. "I was bitten!" Sarah exclaimed as she attempted to get up and almost fell off the bed.

"Sarah, please; not until you've regained your strength." Clive ignored Sarah's feeble protests but assisted her with sitting up in bed.

"Will I become one of them?" Sarah touched the bandages on her wounded shoulder. The burning in her shoulder was intense and her question was fueled more from the movies she had watched than any reality she had come across. In truth, she had never known anyone to survive a werewolf attack.

"No," Clive responded with a relieved look. He got up from Sarah's bedside and began opening the curtains in her room. "A werewolf bite usually kills its victim rather than transforms him; however, Dr. Nemitz is a great healer, so you're going to be just fine."

"How long have I been unconscious?" Sarah asked, squinting as the room filled with sunlight.

"A couple of days." He walked over to the dresser to get Sarah some pain pills and a glass of water. "Healing from a werewolf's bite takes time and…good fortune." He handed Sarah the pills, then pulled his chair close to the bed.

Sarah hadn't entirely forgiven Clive for having kept things from her, but at the moment she was more concerned about getting answers than staying angry with him. "Tell me, Clive, why am I safe in Dr. Nemitz' house when there are vampires and werewolves running free in Hallows End?"

"It's not my place to tell you the secrets of Hallows End," Clive responded somewhat sheepishly. "However, Dr. Nemitz will be here shortly and will tell you everything you want to know."

"What are you, Clive?" Sarah's instincts told her he wasn't human, but she was also quite certain that she had never come across anything like him either.

Clive smiled uneasily and let his gaze fall to the floor. "I'm a wood sprite."

Sarah almost laughed. "A wood sprite?" she asked, again trying to hold back her laughter. Sarah was suddenly picturing Clive in a short skirt and bra made of green leaves.

Clive looked even more embarrassed as he raised his head to look at Sarah again. "Yeah, I know; you probably didn't know that men could be wood sprites, huh?"

Sarah looked dumbfounded. "I didn't even know wood sprites existed." She smiled. Sarah looked into Clive's deep blue eyes and had to admit that she was growing fond of him. He was gentle and kind-hearted, traits she was certain her mother had been attracted to as well in her step-father. It was a nice change of pace from the ego-driven, testosterone-heavy men she typically dated.

"My father brought me here nearly 50 years ago," Clive continued in an attempt to help Sarah move past any stereotypical images of what she envisioned a sprite might be. "The Order had been tipped off to our presence in Sweden so we moved here under the hopes that the tales of a 'town built by a great sorcerer to hide immortals from the outside world' were true."

Sarah got a funny look on her face. "Dr. Nemitz? A 'sorcerer'?"

"Yep." Clive nodded his head. "I don't know much about his life before Hallows End, but I've been told he is the last 'true' sorcerer living. I guess there were more of them thousands of years ago…I'm sure Tom, our Librarian, knows more…" Sarah was about to ask Clive about his father, but hesitated as a sudden sadness came upon his face.

"I'm sorry that I deceived you, Sarah. My father left Hallows End years ago to go back to Sweden to help the rest of our kind. At that time, Dr. Nemitz took me under his wing and treated me as if I were his own son." Clive leaned in toward Sarah and once again took her hand into his.

"When he asked me to keep you safe during your stay in Hallows End…I couldn't refuse; especially after I saw you at the diner that morning. You are so beautiful." Sarah turned her head away, slightly blushing.

HALLOWS END

At that moment, a knock could be heard on the opened door to the bedroom. Both Sarah and Clive looked up and saw Dr. Nemitz standing there in his usual pleasant demeanor. Sarah now understood how it was that Dr. Nemitz had founded the town of Hallows End over eighty years ago. She imagined that sorcerers must be blessed with longer lives just as vampires and werewolves were.

"Good morning," Dr. Nemitz said with a cheerful smile. "I'm glad to see you've come back to us, Ms. Chase."

Clive reached over and gently squeezed Sarah's hand. "I'd better get going," he said, getting up from the chair. "We wood sprites have our gardens to attend, you know." Clive gave Sarah one last smile and wink as he turned and nodded his head toward Dr. Nemitz on his way out the bedroom door.

"Charming young soul," Dr. Nemitz said, referring to Clive as he approached Sarah's bedside and sat down in Clive's chair. "I'm sure you have many questions for me." Dr. Nemitz paused to give Sarah the opportunity to interject, but instead, she remained silent, suddenly angry at his partial truths.

"I'm afraid I don't have time to explain everything as I'd originally planned. Shortly after your attack, Diana was given the task of escorting Elise and Brutus out of Hallows End. Once they were past the border, Diana was to ensure that they no longer posed a threat." Dr. Nemitz looked somberly to the side of the room and stared at the window. "I have not heard back from Diana since that night."

"You sent Diana out to escort two vampires on her own?" Sarah asked.

"Ms. Chase, by now you no doubt surmised that the residents of Hallows End are rather 'special'. It only makes sense that the sheriff of a town filled with 'special' residents would have to be doubly special, eh?" Dr. Nemitz paused a moment to allow for effect. Sarah nodded her head slightly, acknowledging the sense his statement made.

"Diana is a Goddess," he continued, "…literally. She is the last of the original race who brought about the creation of all intelligent life on this planet. Her prowess as a warrior is unmatched."

"Then what's happened to her?" Sarah asked, feeling slightly better now that the pain pills had started numbing the intense burning in her shoulder. Her anger ebbed with the receding pain.

"There's no way that Elise and Brutus could have overcome Diana on their own." Dr. Nemitz paused again, only this time a look of sadness filled his face. "I suspect they may have had assistance. We have many enemies among both the human and what we refer to as the 'immortal' races. Some are in pursuit of the powers your sister Sadeana possesses. Others simply want to vanquish the immortal races entirely."

Dr. Nemitz appeared to be done speaking and Sarah still had a million questions running through her mind. "Is everyone in Hallows End…'special'?" she asked.

"Yes," Dr. Nemitz answered matter-of-factly. "I wish I could tell you more, but you need your rest and I must leave tonight to investigate Diana's disappearance. Tom, our 'Librarian' if you will, can answer any other questions you have. Clive will introduce the two of you tomorrow." He appeared somewhat uneasy as soon as he had mentioned Tom's name.

"I do need to tell you one thing about Tom," Dr. Nemitz said hesitantly. "He's a werewolf."

The hairs on Sarah's neck rose up. "He's on our side?" Sarah asked disbelievingly.

"Very much so. In fact, if anything should happen to me, I have entrusted Hallows End and its citizens to Tom's care."

Dr. Nemitz got up from his chair, then sat down again, as though some heavy weight had landed upon his shoulders and forced him back down. "I never told you how your mother died." It wasn't the first question that Sarah had thought of asking him, but it was the one that mattered most to her.

"Your mother was assisting our Directory of Security at the time, William Luse. While Diana handles everything in Hallows End, we have a small task force that's charged with the security of our residents and all immortals living outside of our town's borders. For instance, if an immortal seeks refuge in Hallows End, it is this task force that meets him in the outside world and then escorts him in."

"Why would my mother want to be a part of that?" Sarah asked.

"I imagine it was her effort to stay connected with the outside world…and to you and your step-father even though she could not physically visit you. Your mother was a very spiritual woman. Perhaps she felt closer to you when she was outside the walls of Hallows End and beyond the magic of the cloaking spell that protects the town."

"How did she die?" Sarah asked. She could feel her body pulling her back to sleep and wanted to know the truth before Dr. Nemitz left.

"A spy from a sect called 'The Order' was captured near the border of Hallows End by our security team. He was being held in the dungeon below the Sheriff's office for questioning and somehow he escaped. He detonated an explosive device comprised of an untraceable chemical agent and silver razor blades. Both your mother and William were killed."

Dr. Nemitz turned back toward Sarah with tears in his eyes. "It was my fault your mother was in harm's way that day, Sarah. It was my decision to hold the spy for questioning rather than execute him. Your mother's death will always be my greatest regret."

He got up from the chair and headed toward the door while Sarah sat on the bed in silence. "There is a statue in memory of your mother in the Garden of Spirits," Dr. Nemitz said as he stopped in the middle of the doorway. "I think you should visit it tomorrow." With that he left the room and Sarah drifted into a dreamless sleep.

CHAPTER 20

Dr. Nemitz made sure to wait until dark before heading out to look for Diana. If she had fallen at the hands of Elise and Brutus, he didn't want a little thing like sunlight getting in the way of him discovering the truth about her killers. Although Hollywood had often painted a false picture of how vampires burned up in the direct sunlight, they were in fact weakened by its rays and thus the majority of their species chose to be nocturnal.

As the hour grew late, he continued to track deeper into the forest, his only means of guidance being his sorcerer's sense and the bond he held with the woman he had loved for nearly 150 years. Both Dr. Nemitz and Diana had been with several other mates over the centuries, but since the time they first met, they knew that the other was the last person they would ever love.

A deep surge of anxiety ran down Dr. Nemitz's spine as he approached the clearing where the demons had attacked Diana. He lowered his lantern slightly as he stared at her motionless body hanging upside down from a tree, bloody and battered. He walked over to the tree, his eyes filling with tears, and waved his hand. The rope snapped instantly and Diana's body slowly levitated to the ground where he kneeled down and held her.

"Your dream's over, Albert," said a voice from the shadows. Dr. Nemitz knew immediately that the voice belonged to Elise. She stepped out from the shadows of the surrounding forest with a dozen demon soldiers and Brutus. "She was one tough bitch!" Elise continued coldly. "Took out the majority of our army, so now we have to wait for reinforcements before we can take the town."

Dr. Nemitz ignored Elise's verbal rant and continued to dwell in his pain as he held Diana. He was ready to die. He had fought for over 1,000 years and he was tired. He had faith that Tom could save the residents of Hallows End and he knew that Sarah would help Sadeana with her quest of stopping the Dark Queen. There was nothing left for him to do.

"Come on, Daddy. Aren't you gonna' say something?" Elise teased viciously.

Dr. Nemitz rose, took two steps away from Diana's body and waved his hand again. Diana's body levitated off the ground and then burst into flames. "That is the way you would have wanted it," he said out loud, referring to the ancient Pagan customs that the gods and goddesses practiced when honoring their dead. Dr. Nemitz then turned toward Elise.

"I don't understand what motivates you, Elise," he said, shaking his head and wiping the tears from his eyes. "and…I'm done trying."

"Are you going to try to kill me now, old man?" Elise taunted, continuing to walk toward him while Brutus and the demon soldiers stood ready behind her. In truth, they were frightened by the sorcerer's powers, and the smell of Diana's burning flesh fueled their fear.

"No." His hands intertwined in front of his body in a non-threatening stance. "I have taken enough lives over the years, some deserving; some not as much. I do not want that to be my last act on this Earth. Instead, my last act will be of forgiveness."

"I don't need your fucking forgiveness!" Elise snapped back as she continued walking slowly toward him. In her right hand she held a black dragon-blade, a weapon of the ancient demons. "You are the one who turned your back on me; on all immortals!" she screamed. "You are the one who was willing to sit with your tail tucked between your legs, hiding in Hallows End, while the Order eliminated every last one of us. Your cowardice is to blame for the end that's coming!"

"I don't understand what you're talking about?" Dr. Nemitz responded, confused.

"William!" Elise blurted out. Her demeanor shifted from fury to sorrow as a single tear formed in one eye. "It was your failure to protect us that led to his death!"

Dr. Nemitz was surprised by William's name being brought up. For the first time in over twenty years he saw in Elise the likeness of the daughter she had once been to him. He closed his eyes briefly and the moment of clarity finally came to him. "You loved him," he proclaimed softly as he now realized how blind he had been to Elise's pain.

For a moment Elise looked like she might open up and allow herself to forgive the man she had once loved as a father. But there was too much anger and hurt in her heart. Elise pulled back her emotions, the tear disappeared from her eye, and a look of hatred returned to her face.

"It really doesn't matter anymore, does it?" She now stood only a few feet from him. "William is in the past, as is Diana. Now, you'll join them." She lunged toward Dr. Nemitz with the dagger in her hand to stab him in the belly.

"What the hell!" Elise screamed as she stepped back in pain. She looked down to see that she was bleeding from the exact spot on her body where she had tried to strike Dr. Nemitz. The sorcerer remained unharmed.

"I'm not going to allow you to kill me, Elise," Dr. Nemitz told her calmly. "I still have enough power to ensure that. I recommend you stop trying as well; it will only cause you more pain."

Elise was furious. She let out an insane howl and lunged at him again with the dagger, this time aiming for his heart. She shrieked and stepped back, this time falling backwards as blood spurted from her chest.

"Elise!" Brutus shouted out and ran to her side.

Dr. Nemitz remained solemn as he stood there looking down upon Elise. "I understand now where your hate stems from. I'm sure your love for William was powerful, just as mine was for Diana. And in some twisted way, I'm sure you viewed taking her life as some kind of karmic retribution for the loss of William. However, the residents of Hallows End don't deserve for you to lead our enemies into their sanctuary." Dr. Nemitz nodded his head toward the demons. "I have already entrusted the defense of Hallows End and my people to individuals who will not allow you to succeed."

Elise was choking on her own blood as she spoke. "Hallows End deserves a leader who can show them how to fight! Who won't cower to the threat of humans! Under my command, Hallows End will become more than just a refuge for cowardly immortals; it will become a beacon of power!" With her last word Elise grabbed a gun from Brutus's waist and fired it at Dr. Nemitz' head.

The bullet flew back from the sorcerer's direction and pierced the skull of Brutus who was still kneeling next to Elise. Brutus instantly fell to Elise's side, a small stream of blood oozing from the front of his head. Elise lay back on the ground, exhausted by her failed attempts to kill the doctor.

Dr. Nemitz sighed with disappointment. "Goodbye, Elise." He turned around and walked toward Diana's burning body, closed his eyes, and allowed his body to fall on top of Diana's. The blaze of the fire shot out twenty feet in all directions, consuming everything in the clearing, but leaving the surrounding trees completely unharmed.

Hours later Elise awoke and looked around. Her body was charred, but the wounds she had incurred during her attack on Dr. Nemitz were slowly healing, as was her burnt skin. She looked to her side and saw that Brutus hadn't fared as well. The bullet in his head had kept him from healing fast enough when the flames spread, so he had turned to ash along with every single one of the remaining demon soldiers. Elise was alone.

CHAPTER 21

Sarah awoke the following day feeling slightly better. She managed to take a shower and brush her teeth, though by the time she'd finished getting dressed she was almost out of breath. After making her way downstairs, she discovered that Sadeana had made them breakfast and was sitting at the dining room table, waiting for her.

"Good morning," Sadeana said, her blue eyes radiating with the same color as the tattoo she had revealed to Sarah on their previous meeting.

"Hi," Sarah managed, sitting down in front of a plate of scrambled eggs, wheat toast and coffee. "Thank you for breakfast."

"You're welcome." Sadeana waited for a couple of moments, not wanting to overwhelm Sarah. "I was hoping we could walk over to the library together today...Dr. Nemitz mentioned that you'd be meeting with Tom?"

"Sure." Sarah finished chewing the bite of scrambled eggs in her mouth and slowly looked up from her plate. "This is weird, huh?" she said with a slight grin. Sarah was still finding it hard to believe that the young woman sitting in front of her was actually her older sister. She looked almost young enough to be Sarah's daughter.

"Yeah," Sadeana nodded shyly.

"So, not to be morbid, but Dr. Nemitz told me about my..." Sarah paused to correct herself, "our mother's death. I'd like to visit the Garden of Spirits and see her memorial on our way to the library."

"Of course," Sadeana responded. There was a long period of silence as the two women continued to eat their breakfast, neither one of them exactly sure as to how to start a conversation with the other.

"You look a lot like her, you know?" Sadeana finally spoke up. "You have the same eyes, the same hair. I was always jealous of you growing up, even though all I had ever known of you was from pictures and the stories Mom told me."

Sarah felt herself becoming emotional and immediately changed the subject. "What's it been like for you to grow up around these 'immortals' all your life? I only just found out that there were such things as vampires and the sort. Even then my only experience with them has been hunting them."

"I suppose it's not been a normal life," Sadeana pondered, "but I'm afraid I don't have much of a concept of what 'normal' is. By the time Mother returned to Hallows End, I was already eight years old and training with Dr. Nemitz. Truthfully, I think I've always viewed him as more of a parent than her."

"Training? Like, sorcerer training?"

"No," Sadeana laughed. "He did try to show me a few things, but I was a horrible apprentice for learning magic. Instead we discovered I had a much better gift; for swordplay."

A look of surprise came over Sarah's face. She was having a difficult time picturing the porcelain doll sitting across from her as a sword wielding warrior. "You're pretty good with a sword, huh?"

"I've become a respectable opponent for my trainer, Josh. You'll meet him soon. He's one of the Guardians."

"The Guardians?" Sarah questioned.

"Tom can do a much better job of explaining all this when you meet with him. But basically the Guardians are a small group of immortals dedicated to protecting…well…me. Dr. Nemitz believes I hold some kind of spiritual energy within me that could change the balance of power on Earth. If the Order were to get hold of me, the fear is that it would mean an end to all of the immortal races. If the Dark Queen gets me instead, it could result in the enslavement of the entire human race and cast the world into an age of darkness."

Sarah remembered what Dr. Nemitz had told her about the Order and their part in her mother's death. "What is this Order?"

"Again, I really should defer to Tom. He's much more educated on these kinds of things than I am. Would you like more eggs?"

Sarah could tell that Sadeana was uncomfortable with answering her questions and decided to discontinue them. Still, she would have preferred to have her questions answered by her sister rather than a werewolf. The two of them finished eating and left for the park. As they neared the small archway that led to the Garden of Spirits, Sadeana stopped.

"Would you like me to wait here for you?" she asked in a gentle tone.

"If you wouldn't mind."

Sarah walked through the Garden slowly as she read the names on the marble statues and took time to appreciate the majesty of what they stood for and the lives that were being honored. Suddenly her breath shortened and shivers began to run uncontrollably down her back. Standing only a few feet away from Sarah was a stone depiction of a beautiful white mare and her two foals; one lay in front of her mother's watchful eye and the other lay safely beside.

LEO CRAVEN

As Sarah read her mother's name on the plaque, tears came to her eyes. For so many years she had wondered what had happened to her mother and why she had left. The answer was nothing short of unbelievable, but that didn't matter to Sarah anymore. She kneeled in front of her mother's memorial and cried for the first time in years.

CHAPTER 22

Sarah and Sadeana walked in silence as they made their way from the Garden to the Library. While questions circled around in each of their respective minds, it appeared that neither wished to burden the moment by asking them.

Upon entering the main lobby, Sadeana pointed out the way for her sister and then took a seat in the reading lounge. Sarah proceeded through the library, looking in all directions at the collections of books and the magnificent art work and sculptures that decorated the massive halls. The ceilings were high and arched with beautiful depictions of ancient gods, goddesses and mythological creatures.

As she walked upstairs and made her way to the back of the library behind the archives, Sarah could make out the words "Janitor" on a worn wooden door. She thought it was odd that Tom would be located in what looked like a janitor's closet. She knocked on the door anyway since this was the way that Sadeana had instructed her to take.

"I'm not here," responded a voice from behind the door.

"Tom?" Sarah said awkwardly through the door. "It's Sarah Chase." She heard someone shuffling around and then approaching the door. A middle aged man with graying blonde hair and a scholarly look opened the door and looked at Sarah.

"Of course, my apologies, Ms. Chase; do come in."

"So you're the janitor, huh?" Sarah kidded, nervously. She found herself feeling uneasy about the idea of trusting a werewolf, despite Dr. Nemitz' reassurances.

"Ah, yes, well, that," Tom fumbled. "I'm not fond of company when I'm doing my research. I can be friendly enough, once you get to know me though." He sat back down at his desk and motioned for Sarah to sit in the spare chair in the room.

"I have to admit," Sarah began, as she sat down in the dusty old chair, "thinking of a werewolf as a friend is a bit of a paradigm shift for me. I've become more accustomed to a kill or be killed relationship where they are concerned."

"Of course you have," Tom replied. "You are, after all, Sarah Chase: vampire and werewolf slayer."

Sarah looked a little embarrassed. "I've never referred to myself like that..."

"Oh, I mean nothing by it, my dear. It's meant to be complimentary. Dr. Nemitz and I have been following your endeavors for quite a while. They're rather impressive, to say the least."

Sarah wasn't quite sure how to respond, considering it was Tom's race she had been exterminating. An uncomfortable silence fell between them.

"So..." Tom said, hoping to get the conversation moving again, "while Dr. Nemitz is away, I am here to answer any questions you have." Tom leaned back in his chair and placed his hands in his lap. "Might I suggest a short history lesson to get us started?"

"Of course," Sarah replied, relieved to have him start first.

"In the middle days of Earth, before the Age of Humans, but after the time of the Gods and Titans (Sarah leaned closer), there existed two great immortal kingdoms, Atlantis and Lemuria. As bitter enemies, these two empires constantly waged war against one another.

During the final year of their rivalry, King Kryon of Atlantis offered terms of peace to Lemuria. Secretly, however, Kryon planned to destroy his enemies with a new 'super' weapon. The Lemurians heard rumors of this weapon and sent their crown prince, Lucifer, under the guise of a treaty attempt, to investigate."

While Lucifer was in Atlantis, he fell in love with the Princess of Atlantis, Navaia. She was more beautiful than any woman he had ever encountered in his own kingdom. Her eyes were blue like the clear sky and conveyed such love and tenderness that Lucifer's heart immediately became hers.

While Kryon was not pleased to see his daughter fall in love with a Lemurian prince, he seized the opportunity. Kryon made Lucifer agree, in secret, to help him destroy Lemuria with the weapon of Atlantis. The task required the assistance of someone from inside his enemy's kingdom and Kryon could think of no one better than their own prince.

In exchange for Lucifer's assistance, Kryon promised the hand of his daughter in marriage. Lucifer blindly agreed to the King's deal, the lives of his own people trumped by his love for Navaia. After he had done his part and Lemuria was destroyed, Lucifer returned to Atlantis to marry his beloved Navaia. However, King Kryon revealed that he would never allow his daughter to marry a Lemurian, and instead had Lucifer imprisoned.

After spending many years in the dungeons of Atlantis, Lucifer successfully befriended the slave race of the humans and helped them to plan the destruction of Kryon's empire. By turning the great weapon of Atlantis against its own creators, Lucifer destroyed the Kingdom of Atlantis and escaped with Navaia."

"Tea?" Tom asked, adjusting his glasses.

Sarah nodded dazedly, struggling to wrap her head around everything Tom had told her.

"With the immortal races having lost their two most powerful societies, the humans took advantage and flourished. Blessed with the ability to procreate quickly, they began to rid the earth of all immortal beings. This period of time became known as the "Cleansing". Even Lucifer and Navaia, who had been granted amnesty, were hunted down and murdered, along with their unborn child."

"Fast forward to a new age of earth," Tom continued. "In 1,500 B.C., Amalya, a member of the small circle of species known as the Lamiai, prophesied that the unborn child of the "Fallen Ones" (Lucifer and Navaia) would be reborn to the Earth and wield 'great power'. When the Dark Queen of the Lamiai, Odessa, learned of the prophecy, she wanted this child for her own. We don't know for certain how Queen Odessa planned to use the child of prophecy, but our guess is it might have something to do with the ancient weapon of the Atlantians."

He picked up his own cup of tea and took a sip. "Any questions?"

Sarah laughed out loud, completely overwhelmed. "Oh, one or two!" she managed.

"Well, of course I left out a few details here and there…" Tom murmured, looking surprised that Sarah wasn't all the way caught up with him.

"So, to start, my half-sister, Sadeana: you guys believe she's the re-born child of Lucifer and Navaia?"

"Hmmm…" Tom collected his thoughts. "I would imagine, coming from someone who's been raised in Western Civilization and believes that Lucifer is some kind of all-powerful Devil, this doesn't sound too promising. But that's not the case at all. Lucifer was simply a being, like the rest of us, who fell in love. His decisions afterwards, though, were probably not the best."

"I should add," Tom interrupted Sarah's thought process, "that your sister is not a direct descendant of the timeline I just explained. You see, about 1,000 years ago, a similar event to your sister's birth occurred where the child of prophecy was believed to have been born; only instead of one child, there were two…twin girls."

Sarah gave Tom the look to go on.

"Lord Artair, Guardian of the Northern Kingdom of Scotland, was charged with securing the child of prophecy (children, as it turned out) for King Malcolm II. However, after an unfortunate string of events, one of the children, Avonmora, died and the other, Keara, was lost to the side of evil. Since your sister bears only the symbol of the Atlantians and not also of the Lemurians, we believe that Keara must still be alive."

"She's over 1,000 years old?" Sarah questioned with disbelief in her tone.

"Yes," Tom said matter-of-factly. "If Keara, the child that bore the Lemurian symbol, ended up in the hands of Odessa, she could have converted the child into one of their own…a Lamiai."

"What is a Lamiai?" Sarah asked.

"The Lamiai is a race of "soul stealers", meaning they can provide themselves with everlasting life by stealing the life force of other beings. A little bit like vampires except without the mess."

"How do you know all of this?" Sarah asked. "I'm no history buff, but I don't imagine this is the kind of thing you learn about on the internet."

"You'd be surprised," Tom said with a grin. "Lord Artair actually kept excellent journals. He became obsessed with finding Keara after her mother died. He was also the man responsible for creating The Order, which had a nobler cause back then. Now, unfortunately, it has become a radical sect bent on eliminating the remaining immortal races."

Sarah felt a little sheepish suddenly in Tom's company since she imagined that was quite a bit like what she had been doing.

"My dear, you are not like them," Tom said, sensing what she was thinking about. "It was a member of the Order who killed your mother and my brother, William."

Silence filled the room. Sarah continued to digest the story that Tom had just told her. He remained quiet as well, lost in his own memories. Finally, Sarah took a deep breath and looked up.

"So, what's next?"

Tom smiled. "Did Dr. Nemitz mention that he'd like you to take his place with the Guardians?"

Sarah's eyebrows shot up, indicating to Tom she had no idea what he was referring to.

"Figures," Tom said sarcastically. "The Guardians are a small group of immortals led by the priest Doran, who's a descendant of Lord Artair. Doran and Dr. Nemitz assembled the Guardians in order to protect the child of prophecy, your sister, Sadeana; and also to discover whatever happened to Keara."

"Sadeana mentioned the Guardians," Sarah broke in. "However, I'm not an immortal. Why would Dr. Nemitz want me to become a part of them?"

"Because the only way for the Guardians to succeed in stopping both the Order and the Dark Queen is to have a human fighting with them. You are to be a symbol of hope that our races can exist without trying to enslave or exterminate each other."

"Ah, so no pressure then?" Sarah teased.

"Sounds a bit 'over-the-top', doesn't it?" Tom responded warmly. "In truth, Sarah, no one expects you to save the world. We're just hoping you might consider helping us to protect your sister."

Sarah took a deep breath. She knew this would be the end of her career as a police detective, and from what she had seen, most likely her life. Sarah had tried to keep the fantasy alive that she would someday settle down, marry some guy, have a couple of kids and live a 'normal' life. However, she had always known, deep within, it was never going to happen for her.

"I'm in," she said.

CHAPTER 23

April 4, 1042 AD - Never had any mortal man journeyed to the Black Peak of the Carpathian Mountains and returned. According to the legends with which Artair had now familiarized himself, the Dark Queen, Odessa, dwelled in the mountains along with the rest of the Lamiai. It was said that Odessa went mad after the death of her beloved husband, Hades. The two had built the Kingdom of Lemuria together as well as given birth to the demon race. After Hades' death, Odessa abandoned her home for the Black Peak where she created the small, but powerful Lamiai race.

Artair looked up from the rolling hillside below. He knew that he was most likely leading his men to doom, but he had to try to save Keara. It no longer mattered to him that she was a child of the prophecy, a supposed reincarnation of a child born of Lemuria. Artair only thought of her safety and of his beloved Tyra whom he was certain was watching him from the heavens above.

HALLOWS END

"Gordan," Artair addressed his friend. "I know you understand what I'm asking of you by following me into the sorceress' domain. Do the other men understand?" He searched Gordan's face for confirmation that what he asked of his men was virtuous and not madness.

"My Lord, you are my friend. These men have left behind both family and home to follow you to the most dangerous lands on earth. They know your heart and they are bound to it, as am I."

"You are my loyal and dear friend," Artair responded as he placed his hand on Gordan's shoulder. "I promise you, this is not madness. We shall rescue an innocent child today or die with honor. If I should not make it…"

"Then we shall enter the gates of heaven together," Gordan interjected.

Artair smiled at his friend's words. He nodded his head and proceeded to lead his men up the treacherous peak. Eventually they came upon a slick and narrow staircase of obsidian that forced them to dismount. Leaving the horses with one of his men, they continued on foot toward a small, intricate entrance into the mountain's side. The entrance was marked with etchings of serpents, the sun and winged demons.

"Light your torches," commanded Artair as he stepped through. Inside was a long, narrow tunnel barely large enough for a full grown man to pass through. Artair despised tight places and shouted back to Gordan and the men to keep their distance. Should they come under attack, they would need room to fight.

Deeper they went into the heart of the mountain until at last they came to a cavern. It had been carved into a great hall with statues of gods, titans and dragons placed all around it. His men filed into the room and circled around one another, wary. There were two adjoining tunnels in front of them.

"Do we split up, my Lord?" questioned Gordan. Artair groaned at the thought. He already suspected a trap was awaiting them and dividing the men into two parties would make them that much more vulnerable.

"No, we'll stay together. I'd rather search each tunnel and go in circles than divide our forces."

With his decision made, Artair led his men into the tunnel on the right. After several twists and turns the men all ended up in the great hall again.

"It's a maze," Artair growled.

"Should we go back and look for another entrance into the mountain?" Gordan asked.

Artair turned back to the original tunnel from which they'd come, but now it appeared to have moved and once again there were two large tunnels to choose from.

HALLOWS END

"The Dark Queen knows we're here," Artair stated. "She is playing games with us."

"Welcome, Lord Artair." An eerie whisper seemed to come from all corners of the hall. "We've been expecting you."

The torches of every soldier began to dim while a soft glow of green light came from above. There was no ceiling of any kind in sight, but as the green light glowed brighter, it became apparent that there were several floors and balconies above them. Artair thought he could see the outlines of white beings moving back and forth above him.

"I seek Queen Odessa," Artair shouted to the green glow above. "Will she present herself so that we may speak face to face?" His hand grasped the handle of his sword tightly though he feared the metal of men would have little effect against the Lamiai.

"It is not an exchange of words that has brought you to the home of the Dark Queen," a deeper, raspier whisper replied in the cool air of the hall. "No...I believe it is your intent to steal that which does not belong to you."

"I seek not to steal, but rather to set free!" Artair responded in anger. "Show yourself and..."

Artair was interrupted by the sudden appearance of a woman in a far corner of the hall. She was naked, except for luminous white paint that she wore like clothing against her lithe body. She bore a sword of Eastern origin in each of her hands which she pointed toward Artair.

"Are you challenging me?" he asked. The white figure nodded her head, though she kept it lowered so that no one in the room could see her face. Her long brown hair was pulled back tightly in a single braid. Artair's men looked at him for a command to raise arms, but he only shook his head and gestured for them to stand down. Most of the men guessed that she was some kind of ghost or banshee that challenged their Lord, but he knew it was worse than that.

"I accept your challenge," he replied, bobbing his head up and down as if trying to encourage himself. Artair drew his sword and took a defensive stance. His palms sweated in anticipation of her attack. For the first time that he could remember, the doubt of victory filled his mind.

"Do not kill him," said the deep, raspy voice. "Only play with him, Natalya."

Artair could hear the ghoulish giggles of invisible Lamiai echo in the hall. He suddenly felt many women's hands all over his body, though when he turned, there was no one. His stomach turned from the sensation of their touch.

"Enough of these games!" he exclaimed. "Fight!"

Natalya's movements were swift and sure. She was far quicker than Artair and much more skilled at swordplay. After a few moments of exchanging swings, Artair knew he was outmatched. He threw his sword to the ground and looked to the shadows above.

"Why do you torture me?" he asked. "It is clear that your assassin is much more skilled than I. Kill me or release to me what you had no right to take."

Natalya took a few steps back and from behind her came another figure. This woman was much taller than Natalya, and wore a transparent white robe revealing a wondrously perfect body.

"I did not steal the child, Lord Artair," she said, moving closer. The soldiers and even Gordan froze with fear, assuming this was the Dark Queen, Odessa whom they now looked upon. She had dark, olive skin, black hair and eyes the color of jade.

"The child was brought to me by the same demon lord who received her from you."

"I did not give the child to Dominious!" Artair growled, though in his heart he knew that was exactly what he had done.

"Lord Artair," Queen Odessa's voice was haunting yet soothing. "I am not the evil Queen you think I am."

"Then give the child to me and allow us to return to our homes."

"Hmmm…" Queen Odessa paused. "I feel there is something present here that is getting in the way of us having an honest discussion."

Suddenly the hall fell into complete darkness as every torch in the room went out. Artair heard the screams of his men as he spun around in circles, madly trying to lend assistance to any of his soldiers whom he could reach. The torment of the dark seemed eternal as Artair helplessly chased the shadows and screams with his sword. Finally, silence filled the room and candles throughout the entire hall were suddenly lit.

Artair looked around at the sunken faces and hollow bodies of his soldiers. They were all dead, sucked dry by the Lamiai. He searched frantically until he found Gordan's body. Artair fell to his knees and grabbed his friend by his lifeless shoulders.

"It won't be long until I join you, my brother," he whispered as he placed his fingers on Gordan's face to shut his eye lids. Artair grabbed the sword nearest him and plunged violently toward Odessa. He stopped, immobilized, however, after only taking one step.

Odessa looked around the room and seemed quite satisfied with the result.

"There now," she said in a calm tone. "I believe we can finish our conversation now."

HALLOWS END

Anger filled the Scottish Lord's veins as he clenched his jaw and tried without success to break free of the Dark Queen's spell that was forcing him to remain still.

"You look at me now as if I'm the one at fault here," the Dark Queen scolded, "yet you are the one who led your armed soldiers into the palace of the soul-stealers. Are you not?"

"You murderous whore!" Artair yelled as he continued to struggle against her spell.

"I suppose you would also blame the lion if you led a group of men into his den?" Odessa asked. "You know what we are and yet you didn't care, did you? You were willing to pay with your men's lives for the prize you sought, were you not?"

The Queen raised points of logic that rang truer than Artair wanted to admit. He stopped struggling and instead began to feel the weight of his soldiers' deaths on his own soul.

Odessa raised her arms and the rest of the Lamiai entered the room. They all wore sheer white robes, with the exception of Natalya, and each looked disgustingly content, having just consumed the souls of so many men. Walking alongside one of the Lamiai was a young girl with dark cherry colored hair and emerald green eyes. She wore a solid white robe and walked right up to the still frozen Artair.

"Who is this man?" the young girl asked as she looked upon him.

Artair's eyes filled with tears and he began to weep.

"Forgive me, please Keara," he said. "Your mother loved you until the day she died. It was not her choice that led you to become a slave here in this Hell. It was my lack of courage and failure as a soldier."

Queen Odessa released Artair from his frozen state and he fell on his knees.

Keara smiled at him. "I am not a slave, soldier," she explained. "I am a Lamiai pupil. On my 21st birthday I will be allowed to take the place of an elder and join the sacred circle of 13. You have not failed anyone. Forgive yourself and die honorably."

Simply seeing Keara alive gave Artair some relief. With the words she spoke, however, he could feel shivers running up his spine. He now understood fully why the Dark Queen had bargained with the demons for the girl. He smiled and released a sickened chuckle.

"So this is your plan," Artair said, staring into the eyes of Odessa. "You wanted the child of prophecy to become a part of your evil circle."

"Again, you accuse us of being evil," Odessa responded, "yet we only desire to survive and prosper, the same as any race."

"At the expense of all others," Artair retorted.

"Says the pot to the kettle," Odessa countered. "Keara will take her place among the '13' when her time comes. I had hoped her sister, Avonmora, would do the same. Alas, it appears we will have to wait for another reincarnation before we can make that a reality."

"Why do you need the children of prophecy?" Artair asked as he shook his head in defeat.

"My dear Lord Artair," Queen Odessa smiled. "For many millennia now, the immortals have had to hide in shame from the humans who once were our slaves. Keara has great power, passed on to her through the spirit of the Lemurians, the race I originally gave birth to. Once I have transformed her and whoever's soul the power of the Atlantians passes on to next, the circle of the Lamiai will help our fellow immortals break free of that bondage and restore the order that was meant to be."

"And I suppose you will then reign as Queen over the entire world?" Artair's despise for the Dark Queen grew with every second he listened to her.

"Something like that." Queen Odessa turned to one of her fellow Lamiai. "Transport him to the dungeon, Marella. We shall keep the brave Lord alive until Keara's 21st birthday. I can think of no other soul that would be better than he to be her first."

Artair lunged toward the Queen in hopes of killing her or dying so as to avoid the fate she had just sentenced him to. Instead, he found himself blacking out and awakening in the darkness of a cell he knew would be his home for the next several years.

CHAPTER 24

Sarah woke up to the smell of fresh coffee and hash browns. "I could get used to this," she thought to herself as she hurried through her morning routine and headed downstairs to join Sadeana for breakfast. Sarah's strength was slowly returning, though she had still been spending more hours asleep than awake these last couple of days.

Both Sadeana and Tom had been staying at the Manor since Dr. Nemitz' departure. Tom rarely joined them for meals though as he was too busy debriefing residents of the pending fate of Hallows End. Tom expected that if Elise had succeeded in killing both Diana and Dr. Nemitz that she would soon be making her move to take control of the town. While many of the residents would choose to stay in Hallows End, Tom wanted to ensure that those who didn't would be able to leave safely.

On her way to breakfast, passing by the den, Sarah noticed Tom sitting at Dr. Nemitz' desk, his head buried in a journal.

"You shouldn't read other people's diaries, you know," she teased as she entered the room.

"Ha," Tom replied, amused. "I was just reviewing the last notes recorded in one of Dr. Nemitz' journals. There's a series of these that date back to the 11th Century. Fascinating reads."

"Which century is that one about?"

"This one is actually the most recent of the journals. It covers the last twenty or so years of Hallows End. Since the good doctor isn't here to record the final entries, I thought I would take it upon myself to do the honors." Tom's face suddenly became somber.

"Do you believe Dr. Nemitz will come back?"

"No," Tom swallowed. "In fact, I'm surprised we haven't seen Elise return yet. It's been two days since he left, and the fact that neither he nor Diana has returned most likely means they're dead…and that Elise survived."

"You and Dr. Nemitz were close?"

Tom took a deep breath and looked at Sarah as he sat back in his chair. "He was like a father to me. Dr. Nemitz saved my brother and me from a village near Tahoe. Many of us Lycans had fled there in hopes of finding sanctuary. However, a Lycan slayer found out about the place and exterminated everyone except the two of us."

"I'm sorry," Sarah paused, feeling somewhat sheepish for having been branded a 'slayer' herself. "What was your brother like?"

Tom chuckled. "You mean, was he an anal-retentive book nerd like me? No, William was a hero. He was the reason we survived long enough for Dr. Nemitz to find us. William was actually Dr. Nemitz' first choice to oversee Hallows End, but after his murder, it was up to me to take over the role."

"Dr. Nemitz told me my mother had been helping your brother. Were my mother and William...?"

"No," Tom stated indifferently. "Actually, your mother seemed to have an interest in Doran, the leader of the Guardians. My brother, on the other hand, was in love with Elise."

Sarah looked surprised at Tom's statement.

"Elise wasn't always the monster she is now," Tom explained. "It wasn't until Williams's death that Elise became hateful and reckless. I don't think Dr. Nemitz ever knew about Elise and William, and I didn't have the heart to tell him since he already felt responsible for William's death. I couldn't bear the thought of the good doctor blaming himself for Elise's dark turn as well."

"And what happens when Elise returns to Hallows End?"

"She'll take over. I'll escort those who want out up north with me. There's a small campground with cabins in the Oregon forests that no one knows about. Dr. Nemitz and I secured the location years ago in case anything happened to Hallows End. It will be a bit rustic, but at least it will be safe."

Tom paused for a moment and leaned over the desk toward Sarah.

"Sarah, I want you to understand that once we leave Hallows End, it will only be you and Sadeana that go with the Guardians. Your quest is too dangerous for anybody else, and I promised Dr. Nemitz that I would protect the residents of Hallows End."

"I understand. I really have no idea still who the Guardians are or what this 'quest' is that I'm supposed to be part of." Sarah looked to Tom for an answer, but his expression remained blank.

"I'm sorry, Sarah, but it's not my place to answer that. Dr. Nemitz left me in charge of protecting Hallows End. Doran's the one in charge of saving the world."

"Well, do you have any advice for me, at least?"

Tom smiled. "Yes. Don't get caught up in the perceived physical 'gifts' of your immortal counterparts. Being an immortal doesn't mean they can't die; it's simply a term used to describe those beings that are not human. And while their bodies age slower and heal faster than yours, you have something that no one else of the Guardians possesses; not even your half-sister."

"And what's that?" Sarah inquired, very interested to hear Tom's answer.

Tom's face went blank. "I don't know," he said shaking his head. "Dr. Nemitz never actually told me...but I'm sure when the time is right, you'll find out."

"Thanks a lot, 'Gandalf'," Sarah quipped, annoyed by Tom's ambiguous comments. Tom looked back at her quizzically, not understanding the reference.

"It's a pop culture reference; forget it. When will Doran and the Guardians arrive?"

"They already have. They're waiting in a cabin just a couple of miles south from here near the border of Hallows End. The cabin was built a long time ago, but it does have a fully stocked armory. However, I need you and Sadeana to remain here in Hallows End until Elise's return. In order to get the residents out safely, I'll need the two of you to create a distraction."

"Great," Sarah responded sarcastically. "I'm pretty sure I can't outrun a lynch mob of pissed off vampires for a 'couple of miles'."

"You'll be all right. I'm not even sure Elise will care that we've fled. Her primary ambition is to gain control of Hallows End and that's what she'll have done."

Sarah thought back to her experience with Elise in Lucifer's Garden and wasn't convinced that the blood-lusting bitch wouldn't try to hunt her down. Unless Dr. Nemitz and Diana made a surprise re-appearance, there was no one to stand in Elise's way. "Shouldn't we send someone to find out what happened to Diana and Dr. Nemitz?"

"I already did, this morning. Hopefully they come back with some news…any kind of news at this point would be good to have." Tom looked down at the journal in his hands and closed the cover. "Would you like to see something?" He got up from his chair and headed over to the large book case on the wall behind him.

"When Dr. Nemitz first built Hallows End, he had a secret basement put in below this house. There's a hand sensor on the side of the shelf here," he said as he placed his hand on the spot he was referring to. It triggered the entire book case to slowly turn away from the wall. "My bloodline, along with Doran's and yours, are the only ones it will recognize."

"Surely Elise knows about this basement?" Sarah asked as they walked down a winding staircase that emptied into an enormous room. She heard the book case slide back into position and a feeling of anxiety came over her as she was left alone with Tom in the pitch black.

"Whoops, sorry about that," he apologized. "Illuminate."

HALLOWS END

As Tom spoke the word, several lamps throughout the basement lit up to reveal a museum of artifacts, weaponry and hundreds upon hundreds of books. "The library has replicas of many of these books, but these, my dear Ms. Chase, are the originals."

Sarah was speechless as she looked around open-mouthed.

"This is the single greatest collection of 'immortals' history that exists. And to answer your question, Elise did know about it, but Dr. Nemitz removed it from her memory years ago."

Sarah slowly took in the scene as she walked toward a wall made entirely of granite with names etched into the stone. "Hercules," she read aloud.

"Ah, yes," Tom spoke as he followed Sarah. "Certainly not a complete collection, but behind these granite tiles lie the remains and ashes of some of the greatest immortals to have ever lived on Earth. Nemindor's circle, Nemindor being Dr. Nemitz' original name, was given the honor of guarding these remains. As the last sorcerer of his circle, and possibly the last of his kind on Earth, it was his responsibility to protect all of this."

Tom let out a sigh and his gaze fell to the floor. "And now I'm afraid it's mine," he said in a quiet voice. "The thought of leaving Hallows End and all of this under Elise's control makes me sick, but I guess I'll have to live with it...for now."

"Do you have a plan for how you'll take Hallows End back?"

Tom half-smiled. "Maybe…but let's see how I do at getting the residents safely out first."

Tom walked over to a book case standing by itself in the middle of the room and placed the journal he had been writing in on the shelf.

"Probably time I join you and Sadeana for breakfast, eh?" he said, making his way back to the stairs.

Sarah began to follow him when suddenly she noticed an unfamiliar symbol glowing on the ring she wore on her right hand. The ring had been given to her years ago by her martial arts instructor, but until this moment Sarah had always believed it to be just a plain black ring. As she paused to gaze at her hand, another glowing object caught Sarah's eye on a small table in front of her.

Sarah walked over to discover an amulet that bore the same symbol as her ring. Almost by instinct, Sarah snatched the amulet and placed it in her pocket.

"Are you coming, Ms. Chase?" Tom asked as he began to climb back up the stairwell.

"Right behind you."

Sarah had no idea why she had stolen the amulet, but she felt as though a strange force from within the room was compelling her to keep the object. In fact, Sarah thought she could almost hear a whisper upon the

stale air saying "keep it; it's yours." After a brief pause,
Sarah snapped out of her trance, and made her way back
up to the den, the amulet still safely in her possession.

CHAPTER 25

There was an uncomfortable mood about town as the end of another day neared without any sighting of Diana, Dr. Nemitz or Elise. Sarah had felt invisible as she made her way from the gym in the morning to lunch with Clive, and then over to the library in the afternoon. No one, other than Clive, had spoken more than two words to her. The absence of the good doctor and his sheriff had truly left the town feeling 'hallow'.

Sarah decided to visit the library in an effort to learn more about the immortal races. She skimmed through dozens of books that covered a wide variety of topics, including the origination of life on earth, the rise and fall of the great kingdoms of Atlantis and Lemuria, and the prophecy of which Dr. Nemitz and Tom had spoken. Sarah found the journal entries of Lord Artair particularly interesting since it was his great grandson, Doran (the name had been passed down to each of the first born in his bloodline), that she would now be joining forces with as part of the Guardians.

HALLOWS END

The sky grew dark as Sarah made her way back to Dr. Nemitz' home to have dinner with Tom and Sadeana. She had become somewhat frustrated with their conversation of late as it was always the same. They would review the plan of escape, down to the finest detail, and then, if Sarah started asking questions about the Guardians or their mission, the conversation would end quickly with an ambiguous response from either Tom or Sadeana.

"How was the library?" Tom asked as Sarah entered the house. Tom had invited Sarah to join him in the basement to read from the books down there, but Sarah was feeling guilty for having taken the amulet earlier that morning. In addition, Sarah still found herself having difficulty with the idea of becoming overly friendly with a werewolf, despite the fact that Tom was about as nice a guy as Sarah had ever met.

"Educational," Sarah expressed with wide eyes as they seated themselves around the dining room table.

As always, the table was set perfectly with silver utensils and fine china that featured small black eagles on the rims of the plates. Tom had mentioned over breakfast that the black eagle was the official coat of arms for Austria, Dr. Nemitz' homeland. This also explained the etching of the large black eagle on the front door.

"Dinner is ready," Sadeana exclaimed as she walked in from the kitchen carrying a large serving dish of spaghetti. She had grown accustomed to cooking for Dr. Nemitz and herself over the years, and continuing with the tradition kept her hope alive that he would return. As she served the steaming plate of pasta and marinara sauce, Tom poured them all wine and they began to settle into their routine of reviewing the escape plan. After about twenty minutes, Sarah's patience had finally come to an end.

"All right guys, enough is enough," Sarah pronounced. "We've got the plan down. When are you two finally going to tell me what the hell I'm getting myself into?"

Tom took another sip of his wine. "My dear Sarah, we're not trying to keep anything from you. The greater part of what motivated Dr. Nemitz to involve you in all of this…he never shared with Sadeana or me. In truth, we know very little other than the fact that he wanted you to join the Guardians and help protect your sister."

"And what of the pending mission of the Guardians that follows after we leave here? You're telling me that neither of you knows what Doran is planning?"

Tom hesitated slightly. "Well, in that case, we do…to a certain degree. The finer details of what Doran and Dr. Nemitz had planned once Sadeana and you left Hallows End weren't shared with us. However, we do know that the Guardians are most likely headed to the Black Peak, which is located in the Carpathian mountain range of Romania."

"To take on the Dark Queen?" Sarah questioned, proud of herself that she was starting to put together the timeline and events that surrounded the prophecy.

"Actually, they were hoping to avoid that; at least for now. Odessa is possibly the most powerful being on the planet. To confront the Dark Queen would mean almost certain death for some if not all of the Guardians. The real purpose of their mission is to try and secure the other child of the prophecy."

"Keara," Sarah said out loud.

"The Guardians hope to rescue Keara from the Dark Queen's clutches so that she may join our side," Sadeana interjected.

"With Keara's help," Tom continued, "the Guardians would have insight into what Odessa's planning. We suspect it has to do with the ancient weapon of Atlantis, but we have no idea how she plans to resurrect it. The weapon was destroyed many millennia ago along with its creators. What we do know is if the Dark Queen were able to yield that kind of power, every being on the planet would be at her mercy."

"What reason do the Guardians have to believe that Keara would join our side?" Sarah questioned. "Hasn't she been one of 'them', the Lamiai, for over a thousand years?"

"Indeed she has," Tom replied. "I'm not going to sit here and tell you that it's a good plan, Sarah.

Unfortunately, I believe it's the only one the Guardians have at the moment."

"Did your scout return with any news?" Sarah inquired before taking another bite.

"He did not," Tom said solemnly.

Suddenly, the front door to Dr. Nemitz' manor burst open.

"Tom!" Clive shouted, trying to catch his breath as he entered the dining room. "Elise is approaching and she has an army with her! A demon army!"

"Sound the alarm and get everyone to the rendezvous spot immediately!" Tom ordered. Clive nodded his head, taking only a brief moment to glance at Sarah, and then left as quickly as he had come in.

Tom turned his attention to Sarah and Sadeana. "Leave now. I'll meet you at the rendezvous point and then tell you where to go from there."

Sadeana and Sarah jumped up from the table and headed toward the back door where they had stored their packs. Tom sat at the table for one more minute as he gathered himself and finished his glass of wine.

"Albert," Tom said out loud as he stared at his empty wine glass. "If you're still watching over us, I would greatly appreciate your assistance in helping our friends survive."

HALLOWS END

He turned his head toward the window and took in the view of the park one last time. The sunlight was fading, an ominous symbol of the pending darkness that was about to consume the town. Every happy moment that Tom had ever experienced had occurred in Hallows End. His eyes began to water at the thought that he might never return.

CHAPTER 26

Elise marched into Hallows End wearing a long black gown with a crimson cape. She grinned confidently with an army of over 100 gray demons following behind her. Now that Dr. Nemitz and Diana were out of the way, there was no one left who would dare challenge Elise. As they crossed over into the downtown area, Tremissa came out to greet them.

"About time you got back!" Tremissa called out to Elise.

"This town is ours now. Have you seen that snithering wimp, Tom?"

"He's been staying up at Dr. Nemitz' house, with that Chase girl."

Elise turned to the Demon general. "That's the Doctor's house," she pointed up the hill about a quarter-mile down the road. "You should find what you're looking for there."

As the general started issuing orders for his men to head toward Dr. Nemitz' manor, Elise grabbed him by the arm. "Take anyone and anything you wish, but leave the damn place intact. That's my house now!"

The demon general glared back at her without a word as he shrugged her off his arm.

"What's with all the boys?" Tremissa asked impishly as she watched the demon army head up the hill.

Elise smirked. "They want something that they think is located in Hallows End. I actually have no idea what it is and they wouldn't tell me. However, they agreed to take out all our enemies for us so I figured, eh, why not, right?"

She started walking in the direction of the store fronts as Tremissa followed behind. "First things first. Grab Martin and go to each residence. Let them know that they're either with us or against us."

"And if against?" Tremissa asked deviously.

"Then they can have a one-on-one with their new Governess," Elise retorted with a horrible laugh.

"What about those who try to sneak out and leave? I have a feeling Tom's been trying to convince a few of the residents to go off with him somewhere, although I haven't been able to find out where they're planning on heading."

"Let them leave," Elise responded, indifferently. "Hallows End will become a powerful stronghold for the immortal races. I don't want any spineless friends of the good ol' Doctor or Tom bringing this town down."

Tremissa was a little surprised by Elise's response, but shook it off as she headed out in the direction of the Spa to retrieve Martin.

Elise turned her attention to the diner. If there was anyone left in Hallows End who could challenge her authority, it was David. Although he was a pacifist these days, Elise had heard stories of his time as a soldier during the Civil War. According to Dr. Nemitz, David had single handedly taken out thousands of rebel soldiers and was instrumental in winning the war for the North.

"Is David around?" Elise asked as she stepped through the front door of the diner. The waitress whom she was addressing, Lucinda, was also one of her servers at Lucifer's Garden.

"No, Miss Elise," she responded timidly. "Dave left in a hurry just a few minutes ago. He asked me if I would close up tonight."

"Good," Elise responded, feeling confident that David had chosen to run away with Tom. "Lucinda, there's a few changes that are going to be happening around here. Why don't you go ahead and take over as the manager of this dump. Tomorrow, let's you and I discuss a re-model."

"Yes, ma'am," Lucinda responded obligingly.

As Elise exited the diner, a demon soldier approached her.

"We didn't find anyone in the mansion," he stated.

"So?" Elise shrugged.

"My general isn't pleased." The soldier remained standing in front of Elise.

"Who are you looking for?" She asked, somewhat curious by the revelation that the demons appeared to be searching for a 'someone', rather than a 'something'.

"That's not important!" the soldier barked.

Elise rolled her eyes, annoyed with the demon's attitude. "Try the library then. Whoever you're looking for might be holed up in there." She pointed him in the direction of the library.

As the soldier went running off, Elise considered the dilemma she'd be in if the demons didn't find whoever they were looking for. They were likely to burn down Hallows End and everyone living there if they discovered that she couldn't fulfill her end of the deal. As to who they were looking for, Elise guessed it had something to do with either the girl Dr. Nemitz had been protecting all these years or Detective Chase.

Elise couldn't imagine what the demons wanted with common humans, but she knew she couldn't afford to simply let Tom disappear with them. She immediately began heading for a small outpost located near the coast line that they had used for keeping an eye on the ocean side of Hallows End. If Tom was trying to lead a group out of Hallows End, that would be the most logical rendezvous point from which to leave.

CHAPTER 27

Tom arrived at the outpost where about thirty residents had gathered. They were all carrying flashlights or lanterns along with an assortment of gym bags, suitcases and backpacks. Expressions of fear and doubt filled their faces, although Clive and David were doing their best to put everyone at ease.

"Is this all?" Tom asked.

"I'm afraid so," Clive responded as he stepped away from the group. "Most of the others were too scared to leave once Elise arrived. Besides, you know, Hallows End is the only home they've ever had."

"I know how they feel," Tom said softly to himself. "Very well, we need to leave now."

Tom turned toward Sarah and Sadeana. "The two of you take the southeast trail for the border of Hallows End. After about a mile and a half you'll come across a large, black granite boulder. Head directly south from there and after a half mile more you'll find the Guardians."

As Tom and the others began to head north, Clive remained standing in the company of Sarah and Sadeana. He looked into Sarah's eyes.

"I want to fight with you," he said. "Only…"

"It's not in your nature," Sarah finished his statement for him. Sarah had gotten to know Clive pretty well during her short stay in Hallows End. He was one of the kindest souls she had ever met, but she could tell that Clive wasn't a fighter.

"I guess it comes with the territory of being a sprite," he joked. Clive moved in toward Sarah for a kiss goodbye. As their lips parted they heard a sudden rush of wind nearby.

"Oh, this is touching," Elise cackled as she appeared from behind a large redwood under the emerging moonlight. Sarah pulled her gun while Sadeana drew her swords.

"The town is yours, Elise," Clive said angrily. "Leave them alone!"

"Grew a pair, did we Clive?" Elise said as she walked toward him. "Isn't it a shame when the pretty ones bother to talk, eh ladies?" Elise glanced toward Sarah, "After all, there are so much better things they could be doing with their mouths."

Clive began backing up slowly from Elise. "What did you do to Dr. Nemitz and Diana?" he asked angrily.

"The same thing that I do to anyone who gets in my way. I killed them!"

Clive turned his attention toward Sarah and Sadeana who were preparing to attack. "Go!" he shouted. "She'll kill you both!"

"Yes, do go," Elise stated as her gaze remained locked on Clive. "The demons will be along shortly and the further you're away from my town, the better!"

"The demons are after them?" Clive asked, confused.

"It appears that way," Elise responded happily. "I admit I was a little disappointed over the fact that I wouldn't get to kill Detective Chase myself…oh well, I guess you can't have it all."

Sarah watched helplessly as Elise continued to back Clive up toward a large boulder. She truly cared for him, but if what Elise was saying was true, Sadeana's and her only chance to reach the Guardians in time was to leave immediately. Sarah looked into Clive's eyes one last time before turning to Sadeana. Both women nodded to each other and then ran in the direction that Tom had directed.

"Guess it's just you and me now, Clive," Elise said, licking her lips. "I wonder if you taste any different now that you've been tainted by a mortal."

"You have what you want, Elise. If you want me as well then, fine. I don't care what happens to me."

"You're right, Clive, I do have what I want." Elise stopped walking, crossed her arms and placed her right index finger on her lips. "Maybe I should let you live and be my boy toy? However," her voice dropped an octave, "if memory serves me right, you chose that human bitch over me, didn't you?"

Elise lunged toward Clive and buried her fangs into his throat, driving him to the ground. He was no match for her as blood gushed from the sides of her mouth. After a few moments, Elise stood back up and wiped her mouth. "Now, you die alone," she said as she began her walk back to Hallows End.

Clive remained on the ground, looking up at the stars in the sky. As he took his last breath, his thoughts filled with Sarah and the love he carried for her. With his eyes closed, Clive slowly drifted away, the image of Sarah and him on the ground of the Garden of Spirits being his last fleeting memory.

Elise was half way back to town when the demon general and his army approached her in a rage.

"We found no one in the library!" the General shouted.

"I know who you're looking for," Elise rolled her eyes at him. "Both the police detective and the cute little blonde with swords are heading south at this very moment. If you hurry, I'm sure you can catch them."

The general didn't confirm her suspicions, but Elise could tell from his expression that she had guessed correctly.

"You better not be leading us in the wrong direction," he growled.

"Honey, I don't ever want to see them or you again," Elise snarled, "so I sure fucking hope you find them."

As Elise neared Hallows End and saw the lights glowing from downtown she grinned.

"It's Mine!" she squealed in delight.

CHAPTER 28

"Hey, Brit," Martin called out from a few feet away as his hand touched his attractive client's hip. "I'm going to be in a personal training session with Veronica for a while. Please make sure I'm not interrupted."

"Yes, sir," Brittany responded as she tipped her head slightly in her best valley girl impression. "You can count on me!"

Martin and Veronica headed upstairs to the private training studio as Brittany turned her gaze back to the front and shook her head. Martin had five or six personal training clients like Veronica and, not surprisingly, none of them were making much progress with their physical fitness. After a few minutes, Veronica's moaning could be heard throughout the entire club.

"Oh, my god," Brittany exclaimed, as she leaned under the front counter to turn up the sound system.

"Hi ya', Barbie," said a sarcastic voice from out of nowhere. Brittany looked up to see Tremissa approaching the front counter. "I need you to get Martin for me."

"Martin's in a personal training session right now and asked that he not be disturbed."

Tremissa popped her neck and let out an annoyed sigh. "I don't care who Martin is fucking right now, get him!"

"What's going on, Tremissa?"

"Listen, 90210," Tremissa snarled, "I didn't come here to socialize. Elise is back and we've taken the town. Unless you want me to leap over this counter and rip off that useless head of yours, you'll get Martin for me right now!"

"But…" Brittany faded out.

"Forget it!" Tremissa snapped as she stormed past the front desk.

Brittany jumped up to cut off Tremissa's path. "I'm sorry, Tremissa, but only members can pass this point."

"What the hell are you talking about? All of the people who live here are members!"

Brittany knew her attempts to stall Tremissa weren't going to work. Veronica had been secretly working on Martin for the past few days to see if he could be persuaded to help Tom, should Elise return. Unfortunately, time had run out, and other than a few orgasms, Veronica hadn't been able to get much of anything from Martin.

"Get the fuck out of my way!" Tremissa yelled.

"You know, Tremissa," Brittany responded, her demeanor suddenly changing, "I don't really care for you, so…I actually don't think I will be getting out of your way."

Tremissa looked back at Brittany in disbelief. "Do you have any idea what I am?"

"A real bitch!" Brittany retorted, dropping her cover as a brainless counter girl.

"You're dead," Tremissa stated coldly. She took two steps back and began to transform into a hellish, bird-like creature. Black wings sprouted out of her back, talons slowly emerged from her hands and feet, and her face contorted into a horrible dark mess of yellow eyes and jagged teeth.

Brittany was aware that Tremissa was a harpy, but this was the first time she had ever witnessed her true form.

"And I thought your pink hair was ugly!" Brittany mocked her.

Tremissa lunged at Brittany, expecting to shred her in a matter of seconds. However, she was quickly proven wrong. Brittany met her with a roundhouse kick that sent the harpy crashing back twenty feet through the front wall of the spa. Tremissa sat up and brushed off the bricks that had crashed upon her.

"What the hell are you?" Tremissa growled as she got up and stalked back into the spa.

"Oh, a little bit of this, a little bit of that," Brittany responded, using her valley girl tone again to egg Tremissa on.

Tremissa went on the attack again, but this time took to the air as she landed one of her claws across Brittany's left shoulder, tearing the flesh to the bone. Brittany winced in pain, but still managed to plant her right fist into Tremissa's jaw, this time sending the harpy flying into the first row of treadmills behind the front counter.

"You know," Tremissa said as she once again picked herself up off the ground. "had I known you weren't just some skinny waste of space, I might have invited you to join us."

Brittany could tell that Tremissa was going to be a more difficult nemesis than she had anticipated. Rather than risk having Martin, or even worse, Elise, come to Tremissa's aid, she decided it was time to end their fight. She quickly moved over to a rack of weight plates and began throwing multiple 45 pound plates in Tremissa's direction. Tremissa dodged the first two, but the third hit the harpy in the head and knocked her out.

Brittany considered going over and smashing in Tremissa's skull while she was unconscious, but she knew her mother wouldn't have approved. "A goddess must always do the honorable thing," her mother had taught her. In truth, Brittany was only half-goddess, but her mother's words resonated with her as she left the spa to meet up with the Guardians.

CHAPTER 29

Sarah's heart pounded as she tried to keep up with Sadeana through the forest. Not only was Sarah's body still recovering from the werewolf bite, but she was also struggling with having just left Clive alone with Elise. She knew it wasn't likely the vampire would spare him.

"We're almost there," Sadeana called back as the cabin came into view. She stopped running and turned to see Sarah trying to catch her breath. Her eyes softened as she gently took a couple of steps back toward her sister.

"I know you feel like you have to be protective and have it all together right now," she said, looking straight into Sarah's eyes, "but don't. I realize I'm still a virtual stranger to you. Everything you've been told over the last few days is probably overwhelming." Sadeana paused for a second. "And, I know you cared for Clive."

Sarah stood there silent. It was true that her experience in Hallows End hadn't been easy to take in stride, but she wasn't about to show any weakness to the sister she was supposed to be protecting, especially when there was an army of demons chasing after them.

"Listen," Sadeana got closer to Sarah, "I know what Dr. Nemitz told you about the Guardians needing you to join us. When Doran and he first assembled the group they swore they'd always have someone representing the human race in it."

Sadeana paused for a minute. "I realize I'm human, but evidently I don't count since I have this magical tattoo on my back," she said mockingly.

Sarah wondered to herself where this was going as they appeared to be wasting precious seconds.

"The truth is, we have a back-up," Sadeana continued. "There's an FBI agent who's been helping the Guardians for a few years now and he could take your place. Dr. Nemitz knew there was a possibility that you weren't going to be up for this. Just because you and I have the same mother doesn't mean you want to join us."

Sarah nodded her head up and down and smiled slightly. "So, you're offering me a 'get-out-of-jail-free card', huh?"

Sadeana stared blankly at Sarah, confused by the reference.

"Listen, I don't have any family or friends, so even though you're still pretty much a stranger to me, you're the closest thing I've had to family for a long time. And as long as you're a part of the Guardians, so am I."

Sarah extended her hand to shake, but Sadeana immediately moved past it for a hug. Sarah was a bit uncomfortable with the gesture, but had to admit it felt nice. Just as they resumed heading for the cabin they heard something hurrying through the forest.

"Someone's coming," Sarah said as she drew her gun and took cover behind a large tree stump. Sadeana drew her swords accordingly and hid behind another tree just a few feet away. They both peered around at the same time to see a young black woman approaching.

"It's just Brittany," Sadeana stated as she came out from behind her tree.

"What are the two of you doing out here?" Brittany asked, quickly glancing in Sarah's direction and then back to Sadeana. "Shouldn't you be inside, preparing?"

Sarah still had her gun drawn and was completely confused. "Who are you?" Sarah asked pointedly.

"Oh yeah, you've never seen the real me," Brittany responded as she transformed into the blonde valley girl whom Sarah had met at the Spa. "This would be the person my mother had me posing as in Hallows End…to keep me safe, of course," she said, annoyed.

Brittany quickly shifted back to the tall young woman with caramel skin and long dark hair they had first seen approaching. "Sorry, but I've got to shift back to me. I've been blonde and perky for over 20 years, and hopefully I won't ever have to go back to that!"

Sarah stared at Brittany and couldn't help but see the similarities between her and another woman she had met in Hallows End. "I don't mean to be assumptive here, but you look a lot like…"

"Yep," Brittany interjected, "I'm Diana's daughter. Mom was a goddess, my dad was a shifter. I got the best of both worlds so they asked me to be a part of this whole Guardian thing. Listen, I can fill you in on my back story later."

Sarah knew the moment called for urgency, but she couldn't stand there and not say anything. "Brittany, I'm sorry to tell you this…"

"I know," Brittany nodded as her eyes temporarily drifted into the dark forest. "My mother and I had a very strong bond. I felt it break a few days ago." She turned back toward Sarah and Sadeana. "But there's no time for grieving right now. Let's go!"

Brittany took off for the old, one-story wood cabin and circled around to the back entrance as Sarah and Sadeana followed. "We don't want to knock on the front door," she called out.

"Yeah, Mason's always the one guarding the front," Sadeana explained to Sarah as they caught up with Brittany. "He's a little 'intense'."

"Are you saying that I'm not?" asked a voice from the shadows. A man emerged wearing all black from head to toe.

"Josh!" Sadeana exclaimed as she reached out to embrace him. Josh was short, about 5'6, and wore two Samurai swords on his back, the same style as Sadeana's.

"You must be Detective Chase," said Josh as he turned his attention to Sarah. He removed the mask he had been wearing to reveal an attractive man in his 30's with wavy black hair and a peculiar skin tone that was almost ash-like. Sarah tried to look natural as she reached out to shake his hand.

"It's all right," he said, noticing Sarah's apprehension. "Everyone has that reaction the first time they meet me. My father was a demon. Usually my kind wears make-up to hide our skin color, but I didn't feel the need to get all 'dolled up' for tonight's festivities," he grinned.

Sarah could feel her right eyebrow rise as she let go of his hand. Even though she'd spent time with a werewolf as an ally, it was still hard for her not to stereotype some immortals as evil.

"Hello, there are demons coming, people," Brittany reminded them.

"Come on then," Josh motioned to the three of them, "we better make sure we're in position for our guests."

The back door to the cabin led through a small utility room and into a large open area that included a kitchen, dining room and living room. The other Guardians sat around the fireplace in the center of the room with their eyes fixed on a figure who Sarah assumed must be Doran.

Doran was strikingly handsome, appearing to be in his early 40's, with long brown hair that fell just below his beard. His eyes were a combination of green and gold that pierced through Sarah as his gaze turned to her. The room became silent.

"My god," Doran exclaimed. "You look just like your mother." Sarah suddenly felt uncomfortable as Doran stared at her. She knew he'd had a close friendship, if not more, with her mother. Doran rose from his chair and approached her.

"The demon army will be here any minute, Doran," Brittany declared.

"I see," Doran's current trance was broken. "I must apologize for my lack of manners, Ms. Chase, but it appears we don't have time for proper introductions." Doran turned and pointed to each of the Guardians with urgency.

"You've already met Mr. Josh Keller, our swordsman extraordinaire and Ms. Brittany Morningstar, the strongest member of our team. The others are Mrs. Marie Keller, our resident Angel; Angelique, our Siren of

Destruction; me, as I'm sure you know, am a Lycan; and standing right outside our front door is…"

Before Doran could finish his statement, a hulking man in a black leather jacket slammed the door open. Sarah recognized him immediately. He was the man who had saved her from being raped and murdered in the streets of Los Angeles, back when she was twenty years old and searching for her mother. Sarah now truly understood just how closely she had been watched over the years.

"Mason," Doran finished his sentence. Sarah stared at Mason, but didn't receive any acknowledgment in return.

"Theyyyy'rrrreeee here," Mason stated with a huge grin.

CHAPTER 30

As soon as Mason had spoken, the Guardians flew into action, gathering their weapons and heading out the front door. Doran immediately took notice of Sarah's current arsenal.

"You're going to need something a little more substantial," he observed. "Demons have extremely thick muscle tissue so pretty much every bullet wound is a flesh wound to them. Their skulls are also incredibly hard to penetrate, like a bear's." Doran handed Sarah a solid black, 12-gauge shotgun with a shortened barrel along with a belt of extra rounds.

"These are exploding rounds and will prove quite effective." Doran looked down at the slight bulge of the knife Sarah kept under her right pants leg. "And unless it's your goal to tickle our enemy," he quipped as he handed her a set of thick, black forearm guards, "you'll want to keep that toy of yours sheathed and use these instead."

Sarah took the metal guards from Doran with a questioning look.

"They're called 'bracers' and they're voice activated. Simply shout the words 'Invictus Maneo' and four substantially sharp blades will emerge. These are highly sophisticated, sensory integrated weapons that will respond only to the wearer."

"What does it mean," Sarah asked as she placed the guards around her forearms, "Invictus Maneo?"

"It means 'I remain unvanquished'. Now, stick close to your sister and both of you stay behind the lines. Your assistance might well be needed, but there's no reason for either of you to stand directly in the heat of the battle. If things get bad, fall back to the cabin and head into the basement. Sadeana knows how to access the secret tunnel. She can lead you to safety."

Both Sadeana and Sarah followed Doran out the front door and stopped just a few feet in front of the cabin. Doran continued walking toward the demon general who stood a football field's length away with his army. The forest was less dense surrounding the cabin, although there were still enough trees to provide reasonable cover. Sarah looked around to see where each Guardian had taken up position for attack, careful not to move her head too much and give anyone's location away.

Doran stopped about ten feet short of where the demon general was standing, with Josh beside him.

"Stand down, traitor!" the demon general growled. Doran had earned the title of traitor among the majority of immortals. They believed he was a betrayer of his own kind by being part of the Order. In truth, Doran was a spy, but only Dr. Nemitz and his fellow Guardians knew his secret.

"Well now, that's not a very kind way to address someone," Doran retorted. "Is someone a bit cranky from their layover?"

"We know the girl is here, Priest," the demon general snarled. He was built like a professional wrestler and it was obvious he was upset as indicated by the shade of red his skin had turned. "Stand aside and let us fulfill our mission or we'll turn you and your friends into buzzard shit!"

Doran raised his right eyebrow toward Josh to signal him for the attack. Demon soldiers were relatively slow. Josh sank several throwing stars into the front line of the demon army before they could react. The stars immediately exploded upon contact with the soldiers' flesh, resulting in limbs flying in all directions and causing major disarray within the demon army's formation.

The attack bought Josh and Doran just enough time to race back to the cabin as the demon general reassembled his army for their charge. Marie, aka "Angel Eyes", positioned herself on the roof as a sniper while Mason, Angelique and Brittany remained on the front line with Doran and Josh. The Guardians, though well trained, had never actually fought a battle on open ground. Doran prayed they were ready.

The swarm of giant red soldiers running toward them had Sarah immediately questioning her ability to protect her sister. She cocked the shotgun in her hands and began firing. The kickback on Sarah's weapon was so intense that it took all of her strength just to remain upright.

Meanwhile, Sadeana remained poised with her swords drawn to Sarah's left. Although she wanted to help, Sadeana made no move to advance from her position, knowing she was too important to their mission to risk joining the others on the front line.

The next several minutes were a blur. Brief glimpses of the other Guardians fighting appeared in and out of Sarah's periphery vision as she continued to fire rounds into the hulking flesh of demon after demon. She was reloading her weapon when a large axe suddenly flew in her direction. Sarah ducked in time, but her rhythm broke long enough for three soldiers to close in on her and Sadeana.

"Invictus Maneo!" Sarah shouted as she dropped her gun and prepared to launch herself at the incoming demons. However, there was no need. Sadeana had moved in front of Sarah and with three quick movements of her swords, disposed of all three. Sarah had never seen anyone move so quickly and gracefully. It was like Sadeana was part of the air herself.

The battle didn't continue long as the demons found themselves grossly outmatched.

"Dispense with the rest; we don't have the luxury of being merciful today," Doran ordered. A few of the Guardians chased after the remaining demon soldiers who retreated north into the denser part of the forest.

"I trust you're all right," Doran asked Sarah as he made his way to the front steps of the cabin and sat down to rest.

"It appears you guys didn't really need much assistance from a human."

"On the field of battle, no," he answered matter-of-factly. "But you weren't recruited for your fighting skills."

"Oh," Sarah replied, her pride taking a slight blow from Doran's statement. "Just why am I here then?"

Doran looked up, his face smeared with demon blood. His eyes traveled over to Sadeana's for a moment and then made their way back to Sarah's. "I suppose that's a question that should be answered now."

Doran stood up and took a deep breath. "I'm sure you're already aware we plan to travel to the Black Peak, the home of the Dark Queen." Sarah nodded her head.

"What neither you nor your sister have been told though is what our true mission is once we get there." Sadeana's eyebrows furrowed.

"Contrary to the fairy tale that might have been told to the both of you, our mission is not to save Keara. Both of the twin children of the prophecy lost their souls over a millennium ago. However, the Dark Queen's magic prevented the rebirth of Keara's soul in this new age."

Doran began pacing in a small circle around both Sarah and Sadeana. "The mission of the Guardians is to travel to Odessa's labyrinth, destroy Keara and channel the spiritual DNA she still carries into a new vessel."

"A vessel?" Sarah questioned. "You mean Sadeana?"

"Your sister already channels Avonmora's DNA, proven by the symbol of Atlantis on her skin. And, it's clear by the events of the past that the spirits never meant for only one soul to bear this burden of foretold power."

Chills ran down Sarah's spine as Doran stopped pacing and looked directly into her eyes.

"You, Sarah Chase, are destined to be the other half of the prophecy."

About the Author

Leo Craven is a married father of two, an author and song writer who lives on the beautiful Central Coast of California. Although he disguises himself as a marketing professional, in secret he roams through fantasy worlds, lives among mystical creatures and dares to keep an open mind to the mysteries of the universe.

Throughout his life, Leo has always been drawn to the magical world of movies, graphic novels and books. There is no greater adventure, he believes, then the one that can be had when the mind is absorbed within the world of a brilliant story teller. Countless masterpieces have inspired him, though Tolkien's "Lord of the Rings", the original "Star Wars" and Bram Stoker's "Dracula" he counts among his favorites.

While he also has a passion for both science fiction and horror, it was the character of Sarah Chase that prompted him to focus on the fantasy genre for his first full-length novel (Part One of the "Prophecy Trilogy"). He believes the world of fiction is in need of strong heroines, and Sarah Chase is more than willing to be that champion.

Stay up-to-date on the latest short stories and novels by Leo Craven at www.leocraven.com.

Printed in Great Britain
by Amazon.co.uk, Ltd.,
Marston Gate.